To Tom and

Ann Mann has enjoyed an eclectic career in show business and the media. As a singer, she made numerous broadcasts on television and radio in the sixties and performed in some of the top cabaret spots in the West End of London. She has produced and presented over a 1,000 programmes for TV and radio, worked for Walt Disney and Hammer Films, and lectured on musical theatre and Irish Literature. Her last novel *The Impersonator* received five stars on Amazon and excellent reviews. It is currently being considered for a feature film.

Best wishes
Ann M

Arcanum

AN IRISH MYSTERY

ANN MANN

Matador
9 Priory Business Park,
Wistow Road, Kibworth Beauchamp,
Leicestershire. LE8 0RX
Tel: 0116 279 2299
Email: books@troubador.co.uk
Web: www.troubador.co.uk/matador
Twitter: @matadorbooks

ISBN 978 1785899 799

British Library Cataloguing in Publication Data.
A catalogue record for this book is available from the British Library.

Printed and bound in the UK by TJ International, Padstow, Cornwall
Typeset in 11.5pt Aldine by Troubador Publishing Ltd, Leicester, UK

Matador is an imprint of Troubador Publishing Ltd

Acknowledgements:

John Gale, Yvonne Antrobus, Kate Greer, Paschal Walsh,
Christy Evans, Robin McCaw, Niall Buggy, Declan Kiberd.

★

...The measure of her flying feet
Made Ireland's heart begin to beat;
And Time bade all his candles flare
To light a measure here and there;
And may the thoughts of Ireland brood
Upon a measured quietude.

"To Ireland in the Coming Times"
W. B. Yeats.

COUNTY CLARE.

EIRE. 1735.

Inside the bed, the old man's hair spread out on to the grey pillow. A silver aureole, framing the dull, grey pallor of a dying face. Eyes, rheumy yet still seeing, would not move from their focus.

The candle wisped a grey coil towards the grey ceiling and was instantly rekindled.

A purple, velvet coat braided with silk ribbons of anything but grey hung on the door. Hues of cerise and acquamarine, sherbert and emerald belched almost obscene and forbidden colour into the dismal surroundings. A scarlet, plumed hat with a purple feather hung over the coat, caricaturing a thin, bent figure frozen in time.

The woman holding the candle peered closer at the old man searching for signs of life. She looked older than her fifty years, her hair flat and lank fringing a sallow face that housed two large moles on either side of her chin from which grey hair sprouted eagerly.

She stepped on to something that snapped and lowered the candle towards the dusty floor. A flash of brass buckle on fuschia ignited her wrath and she swore as she kicked it into its companion under the bed, the toes of the battered shoes curling upwards as if pleading for mercy or at least to be worn and danced in again.

"Ifreann na Fola!"

As she cursed, the sound of the door opening spun her round and she released a tremor of relief on seeing a shadow stretching in front of a glimmer of moonshine.

"Tar isteach." ("Come inside")

The figure moved into the candle's light as the woman greeted him, her hand coyly half-covering her mouth to hide the absence of teeth.

The boy was tall, in his late teens, with a mass of red-gold curls which resembled a halo against the gloom. His face was angular, his eyes the palest of blue with lips a little too prominent to create a truly handsome countenance. He was wearing a rough grey shirt and baggy brown trousers. A scarf which had once been red was knotted around his throat.

He stared at the old man who stirred slightly but who kept his gaze on the clothes behind the door. The boy followed his gaze then took down the coat and hat and slowly put them on.

The woman beckoned him towards the shoes which were just visible beneath the bed and the boy stooped to retrieve them. When the outfit was complete, a transformation occurred within the room. The clothes he was wearing seemed to vibrate with an energy all of their own, illuminated by a harvest moon now curious and beaming through the gauzy window pane.

The old man shifted into an almost upright position and focused on the boy who began to twirl and dance around the bed in an orgy of colour and rhythm.

A bony hand extended to draw him closer to the bed and as the boy obeyed the command he bent his head to listen to what the old man had to say.

The words were pithy and urgent and he wasn't quite sure in which language he was hearing them. They took on a resonance seemingly impossible from such a frail body and in an unfamiliar dialect that appeared to pervade the whole room with its message.

"This is all I have to bequeath so use the gift wisely.
Continue my work with diligence or the darkest of evils will descend upon you
leaving those who are deprived of the gift, sorrowful and joyless for all eternity."

The old man then called on all of his remaining strength to reach for something beside the bed. His breath rasping in his throat and with spittle foaming on his lips and chin, he found the item and thrust it towards the boy.

Catching the silver-topped cane with a look of pure delight the boy held it high above his head for a few seconds then brought it down on the wooden floor with a thud, then again harder and louder, finally conjuring up a beat to which he danced. And danced.

Now he was ready.

★

THE OLYMPIA THEATRE
DUBLIN. 2015.

Silas Murphy had learned to ignore the trickles of sweat that fermented in his hairline before snaking their journey down towards his throat and high starched collar. He had also learned to keep the smiling mask in place as he gazed out at the crowd whose standing ovation was now lasting almost as long as the closing routine. The ten positions of the Celtic cross as conceived in the Gaelic version of the Tarot cards. A choreographic tour de force that had almost cost him his sanity when putting it together, but which had received rave reviews and heralded sell out performances for the rest of the tour. It had also cemented the name for his new troupe for which he had been searching for a year. Arcanum.

Now the encore was turning into a ball-breaker after two hours of high-stepping slip jigs, tap, soft shoe and even a traditional hornpipe. Catching Clodagh's eye Silas noted that the bright smile she had been wearing had vapourised, its radiance replaced by a wincing grimace which signalled a warning to his brain that she had almost certainly sustained an injury.

He couldn't afford that. None of them could afford that. Not now.

Clodagh was irreplaceable and the bus waiting to take them on to Ennis that night to begin performances in the town the following day was already parked outside the theatre. The billboards screamed with the critics' praise. "Brilliantly innovative", "Takes the Irish dance to new heights", "Possibly the most mysterious and poetically Celtic of all Irish dance routines."

More bookings, more money and more recognition. Maybe next year they would be filling the 02. That was what he had been striving for since arriving in this city from Boston in 2011, slavishly devoting every minute of his time and scant finances to perfecting the dream. And now that it was within his grasp he couldn't afford to lose it. Whatever the cost.

Pushing himself on towards a second encore, for the audience wanted not just their pound of flesh but the blood, sweat and tears that accompanied it, Silas saw his partner and leading lady wave to the crowd and limp off into the wings. He wondered how serious it was and whether they might have to postpone tomorrow's opening until she had recovered. He could put Sinead on for her, but it would certainly disappoint the punters, for Clodagh was their new Jean Butler. The tall, red-haired beauty with the fiery feet they had all paid for and expected to see.

He stared defiantly into the snow-blinding glare of the arc lamp and flung out his arms, continuing his lap of honour between the erect lines of his twenty-four dancers, his ears buzzing from the frenzy of cheers and applause, his feet lightly skimming the surface of the stage, heels and toes clicking and landing with the precision in which he had been schooled and had re-defined for himself.

When the curtain fell and they were finally allowed to leave the stage, he manoeuvred his way through the excitable cast towards Clodagh's dressing room. The door was open and she was sitting with her eyes closed, her hair still braided in the style of the High Priestess, her blue silk skirt lifted while Justin, their regular physio held her leg in one hand and pressed her swollen calf with the fingers of his other.

For an unexpected microsecond Silas experienced a burning thrust of jealousy then stifled it immediately. No time for complications like that. He may examine those feelings in another place at another time but now there were more urgent matters than affairs of the heart to attend to.

"Don't tell me," he said, closing the door behind him and silencing the other voices. "You've pulled a muscle."

Justin took a roll of bandage from his bag and began to apply it deftly to the swollen leg. "Sorry Silas. I think it's a tear. At least that what it feels like to me. She'll have to go for an MRI in the morning just to make sure."

"I'll be alright." His wonderful girl told him, reaching for a bottle of water and taking a deep glug. "I'm sure I'll be able to work tomorrow."

Silas loosened his collar and unbuttoned his dark waistcoat realising he must stink worse than a rotting trout in Molly Malone's basket.

"When did you do it?"

The bandage applied, Clodagh turned to unbraid her hair which glinted like polished copper as it loosened onto her shoulders and she addressed him through the mirror on her dressing table. "That front click just after the double spin."

"In the Pentacles section when the tempo changed." Silas nodded. "I thought that's when I saw you go". He moved towards her, placing his hands on her shoulders. "You have to get it checked. I'll come with you."

She screwed up her fine features in concern. "Not possible. You've got to take the bus."

"It's alright." He told her. "I'll see them off and ask Terry to take the rehearsal and Michael to deputise for me until we arrive later. I can hire a car and we'll drive down after we've been to the hospital."

Terry the touring stage manager and Michael the head boy dancer were more than capable of checking the dancers into their accommodation and starting the afternoon rehearsal without either of them being there.

"I can take her." Justin volunteered. "If you want to go with the company?"

"No, that's fine." Silas heard himself snap. "If you could make the appointment I'd be grateful. You can come down with us in the car or catch a train if you'd prefer."

Justin closed his bag and made for the door. "I'll accept the lift, thanks. And I'll text you with a time for the appointment. Good night Clodagh. And keep that leg up won't you?"

"Thank you so much, Justin," Clodagh smiled winningly. "See you tomorrow."

When he had gone, Silas flopped into the chair he had vacated and rubbed his thick dark hair, which, with its combination of sweat and gell, resembled that of a demented porcupine.

"I'm sorry." She said softly, starting to remove her make-up with a large wad of cotton wool. "It's the last thing I wanted to happen."

He stretched out his legs and grunted. "I know. But it's not your fault, just one of those occupational hazards. Can I borrow your cell?"

"Sure." She nodded towards an enormous patchwork bag that lay on the floor. "You'll have to switch it on."

"I'd better text the boys and Sinead to warn them. Then I'll clean up and go down to the bus."

He punched out a generic text then slid the phone back on to the dressing-table. "And I'll get a cab to take you home."

A soft drizzle touched the night air as the dancers piled into the tour bus, dragging their wheelie cases and balancing boxes of pizzas and soft drinks with the dexterity of circus performers.

Silas allowed himself a metaphorical pat on the back for locating this forty-five seater for it was the Rolls Royce of the coach world. Executive premier with leather upholstery, a WC and enough room for carrying their luggage as well as the numerous costumes. He had been so used to this size of transportation back home and still found it surprising that the coaches all seemed so small in Ireland, many of them still without air conditioning. But after a long search online and through a mate who was a fan of the show and worked for the local Mayor's office, he had found the ideal firm who provided this sleek black beauty he was now admiring and he reassured himself it was worth every euro in the budget.

"So you won't be coming with us then?" A gravelly voice enquired, interrupting his musings.

The coach driver was probably in his fifties. What hair he had left was a suspect tangerine and a faint purple mottle was creeping into his cheeks. He was smoking a cigarette which had sprinkled ash on to the lapel of his black uniformed jacket.

"No." Silas replied. "An emergency I have to attend to."

The driver nodded towards the coach which was now filled with hungry young people already digging into their greasy dinners. "I thought someone would be in charge."

"In charge?"

"They're a lively bunch. I hope they'll settle down soon and don't make too much mess with that food."

Silas wanted to say 'Wait a second, they've just called on every ounce of their human resources for a relentless two and half hours. They need to come down from all that adrenalin." But knowing that the man wouldn't have a clue as to what he was talking about, he decided on "Don't worry. They'll probably fall asleep by the time you get on the M.18."

The driver maintained his dour expression and appeared unconvinced. "And I'll be looked after when we get there?"

Silas felt his mouth harden. He had just given Terry the twenty-five euros as a tip for the service he had already paid a great deal of money for.

"You'll have your tip. Just get them there safe and sound."

The man grudgingly decided to accept his assurance and clambered up into his seat, turning to give his boisterous charges a less than pleasant glare before revving up the engine.

The rain was falling more intensely now, creating puddles

which reflected the massive dual LED headlamps as they beamed their way out of the theatre car-park.

Silas waved at the figures inside which became mere silhouettes the further they glided from his gaze.

"See you tomorrow." He called, but his words were drowned by a sudden roll of thunder and a streak of lightning that crackled across a blue-black sky.

★

Clodagh had a disturbing dream that night. Maybe it had been the painkillers, but when dawn broke and gleamed a golden filter through the linen blind, her heart was pounding so loudly she thought at first it was a workman hammering outside her bedroom window.

She had been climbing a steep hill that was arduous and seemingly never-ending. At the top of the hill was something resembling a temple bathed in the silver light of the full moon. She was wearing the ivory silk nightgown she had gone to bed in that night with the small gold cross on its fine chain still around her neck and which she tried never to remove, for her faith was an important component of her daily life.

The temple appeared semi-translucent as if made of crystal and as Clodagh moved closer towards the arched entrance, it struck her as hauntingly familiar. Then she realised why. It was a replica of the set used in the Tarot opening and closing of the show. One black and one white pillar framed a tapestry covered with fruit and sheaths of corn. She had been told that the initials on the pillars, B on the black and J on the white were of the names of spiritual guides who guarded the Temple of Solomon. She had forgotten those names now because they seemed to hold no relevance to her understanding of the character and the dance.

As she absorbed these thoughts, the figure of a woman began to slowly materialise. Seated with closed eyes and in flowing blue robes, her form took on an almost three-dimensional air as she drifted towards the dreaming girl.

Clodagh gasped in alarm and found herself making the sign of the cross.

"Holy Mary, Mother of God!"

But the woman wasn't the blessed Virgin. Despite her fear, Clodagh was bound to take a step closer only to realise that the face she was looking at was her own. It was herself wearing a longer version of the costume she wore in the show depicting the figure in the Major Arcana of the Tarot. The High Priestess.

She, the woman, opened her eyes and smiled gently. "No, Clodagh, I am not Mary but I represent the spiritual independence that you seek. I embody all that is feminine and intuitive and empowering."

Clodagh struggled in her dream to understand. "But you're a. ..Pagan figure of mythology and I'm a Christian."

Her own voice answered in a tone that was stern but kindly.

"I understand why you worship Mary. She is a wonderful role-model in many ways, but she is empowered only by men. Impregnated by a man and giving birth to a man. That is what you worship her for. Think, Clodagh. Understand only what you can see and feel. Above you is our lady moon. The female symbol that controls our bodies and our souls. Our twenty-eight day cycle, the waxing and waning of our moods, our dreams and our secrets. I am only saying 'trust your intuition rather than what you have been taught to obey.' This way you will find the secret key to your hopes and fears and be able to unlock the mysteries which lie ahead. "

"What mysteries?" Clodagh asked, her mind a tangle of sleep-jumbled emotions.

But she, the High Priestess was dissolving rapidly into a blue mosaic of tiny lights, and her final words brought Clodagh out of her dream. "Connect with your inner Wisdom for therein lies the path to Enlightenment."

Her heart was beating less rapidly now as the sweet song of a blackbird jolted her back to full wakefulness. How strange was that dream? Did it hold some deep significance that she should strive to understand?

She turned over and reached for her mobile. Unplugging it from its charger she was surprised to see several texts from Silas. "Ring me. It's urgent".

"Ouch!" She'd forgotten her swollen leg as she swung out of bed and checked the time. Six-thirty. Anxiety lodged in the pit of her stomach. What on earth could be so urgent at this hour?

★

Once the wild storm had subsided, Silas fell into a composed and dreamless sleep. He had set his alarm for eight knowing that Justin would probably be unable to fix an appointment before ten and planned to take croissants and coffee over to Clodagh before they left for the hospital.

When his phone rang for the first time at five-thirty, he was sleeping so deeply that it only vaguely registered behind the filmy curtain that covered his consciousness. When it rang again, this time seeming more urgent, he cursed and groped for it in the darkness, finally growling an incoherent hello.

It took him a few moments to register what the woman from the hotel in Ennis was saying and, aware that he sounded as thick as the Dublin Bay mist, he repeated everything parrot fashion while trying to think of an intelligent response to her questions.

"Not arrived. What do you mean, not arrived?"

"Sure, they should be there by now. Three hours ago they should have been there."

"Sure, yes. I'll make some calls and get back to you. Ring me as soon as they turn up."

He rubbed the sleep from his eyes, his body craving the sweet dark allure of caffeine. Before that though he knew he had to gather his racing thoughts into some kind of order. Try not to panic. There must be a logical reason why his troupe had not yet reached the hotel and the first obvious one was that the bloody coach had broken down.

"God," he spat angrily to an empty room, then located Terry and Michael's mobile numbers. "If I've paid all that money...."

He shook his head in bewilderment as the message displayed on both numbers read 'Unable to connect.' Then he tried Sinead and a similar message was repeated. The dancers' numbers continued to roll up before him and however much he had told himself to stay calm, panic now rose in his throat with a wave of nausea.

Sean.....'Unable to connect,' Sarah.....'Unable to connect,' Danny...'Unable to connect,' Val, Cheryl, Maureen, Sam....his fingers stabbed like an automaton upon a phone now damp with perspiration. Not even a recorded voice asking the caller to leave a message. Nothing but those three intractable words which were striking a deep chill in his heart.

He realised it might be an idea just to take five minutes, make some strong coffee and think...

Pacing his small kitchen while the jug bubbled and the first shaft of dawn light pushed its way through the leaden clouds, he tried the office of the coach company. Only an answering service. No surprise there. Perhaps he should ring round the hospitals, but in which area? Similarly the police, but where? And surely to do this was a last resort and a total over-reaction.

Silas took his coffee into the sitting room and opened his lap-top, scouring the local map routes for any reports of accidents between Dublin and County Clare. Nothing major showed up immediately. He scrolled down and checked another site. One motor-cycle casualty at just after midnight on the motorway, a few road-works as always, then something caught his attention and he enlarged it, his tired brain hungry for more information.

An accident between a lorry and two cars at around 1.00 am had partially closed the M18 to Ennis. As he read again slowly Silas experienced the dual sensation of relief and despair. Relief because a coach wasn't mentioned but despair that he was none the wiser. Would they have taken that route? The possibility presented itself that if they had and the M18 had been partially closed, then the driver along with others would have gone off the motorway, in other words diverting through some pretty dense countryside. The timing was about right and this was all he had to cling on to for now.

He checked his watch and downed the rest of his coffee. If that prick had taken any stupid chances and put the coach in danger he would swing for it. He hated waking Clodagh, particularly as the painkillers Justin had given her would have surely knocked her out, but there was no-one else with whom he could share this unwelcome information.

★

She stood in the kitchen of her flat and gazed at Sinead's favourite mug, trying not to let shadows of gloom invade her mind.

When Silas had told her that the coach hadn't arrived, she wanted to believe it was just another dream. It all sounded so surreal and she tried frantically to search for an explanation but kept returning to the vision of some ghastly accident where the coach had overturned and the broken bodies of her friends and her flat-mate were strewn across some darkened road.

She ran the shower and although hampered by her bandage washed as best she could. Pulling her long hair back with a rubber band she knotted it into a pony tail, slipped on an old pair of grey jogging bottoms and a black T-shirt and rubbed her face vigorously with moisturiser. Peering into the steamy bathroom mirror she became unsettled by its pallor and added a brief hint of blusher to her high cheekbones.

Now she waited with tense anticipation for Silas, hoping that he would bring some news of the dancers' arrival in

Ennis, but when she opened the door to greet him she knew from his expression that he had nothing further to impart.

"I've spoken to the coach company." He told her, brushing her face with a distracted kiss. "They've heard nothing. They're going to ring the Garda and the other emergency services and keep in touch with me."

He followed her into the kitchen where she offered him coffee and breakfast which he declined.

"We ought to eat. Keep our strength up."

"I can't reach them, Clodagh. Not one of them"

She abandoned the soda bread she had taken from the cupboard and sank on to a small Perspex chair looking up at him. He seemed to have aged since last night. "Neither can I. What do you think has happened?"

He shook his head, pulled up a matching chair and sat beside her. "I wish I knew. I just don't understand. They should have been there hours ago."

She reached out and touched his arm. "Don't worry, there's bound to be a simple explanation. They can't just have disappeared. I think they've broken down in some country spot which is out of range."

He found himself squeezing her hand which he continued to hold. "So do I. At least that's what I want to believe."

"Do you think we should check on Facebook and Twitter? A long shot I know, but just in case any of them have put anything up in the last few hours?"

"It's worth a try I suppose. You take the girls, I'll do the boys."

An atmosphere of intense silence descended on the bright room as they began to search the dancers' social media sites. After fifteen minutes, the ticking of the Micky Mouse clock on the mantelpiece and the buzz of early morning traffic began to intrude upon that silence, and they met one another's eyes questioningly, each hoping for the other to provide some sort of clue to the mystery that had presented itself.

Silas spoke first. "I've found nothing for the last twenty-four hours. You?"

"Nothing. The latest entries are from five of the girls two or three days ago. Nothing since."

At that point, a text tinkled on Silas's phone which he scanned with urgency, then grimaced.

"It's from Justin. I'd forgotten all about your hospital appointment. It's at 10.30. I suppose I should tell him, but I'll do that at the hospital. I ought to keep the cell free for incoming calls."

The MRI showed that Justin's prognosis had been correct, although it could have been worse. A Grade One tear was how it was described and the doctor suggested staying off the leg for at least a week. She told Clodagh that physiotherapy was essential to her recovery and that she should rest her leg as much as possible.

As the three of them left the hospital there was only one thought on their minds and it wasn't Clodagh's injury.

"I'm going to hire a car as planned." Silas told them. "I feel pretty useless sticking around here and I know they'll turn up in Ennis eventually."

"I want to come with you." Clodagh told him. "Even if I can't dance I want to be there."

"Count me in then," added Justin. "I can't be your physio if I'm in Dublin."

There was somewhere Silas wanted to visit before setting off and that was the headquarters of the coach company to meet the manager whose name was Conor Ferguson. He was a large man with tightly combed salt and pepper hair and matching stubble, wearing a suit which seemed too small for his broad frame. He greeted the three of them anxiously, ushering them into an office where a thin, peroxided woman of about forty was talking loudly on the phone.

"Come in and tell me what you know," he said, waving them towards a leather sofa which had seen better days. "I can't make head nor tail of this."

They squeezed together on the sofa and Silas explained that he had seen the coach off at approximately eleven-thirty the previous night. The journey to Ennis was anticipated as roughly three hours and the hotel had been expecting them to arrive around two-thirty to three a.m. He told Ferguson that he had tried every one of his dancers' cell phones and they were all unavailable.

The woman finished her conversation, scratched her brassy mane of hair and offered them coffee which they accepted like desperate junkies. Ferguson stood behind the desk, too nervous and fidgety to sit, his jacket having been discarded and exposing an ample belly that protruded over his tight trousers.

"Same here. Can't get the feckin' driver to answer. I dunno what the feck's happened but I've been speaking to a Detective Superintendent Joe Tierney at the Garda. He's okay but they've got this beaurocratic crap which is holding everything up, like, should it be traffic division or missing persons? Anyways, as soon as they've sorted themselves they'll be alerting the police, hospitals and break-down services between here and County Clare. I'm waiting to hear back. Bloody mystery if you ask me!"

"Do you know what route they would have taken?" Silas enquired as the coffee arrived and was distributed.

A map was already laid out on Ferguson's desk and he loosened his tie as he followed with his finger the map lines while the others craned forward.

"I'm pretty sure they'd have gone on the motorway up to the toll at the Shunnel."

Silas looked puzzled so he elaborated.

"Oh sorry, the Shannon/Limerick tunnel. Basically, my driver would have taken the M18 to Ennis. Pretty standard stuff since the dual carriageway has been extended. We know there was a crash between a lorry and two cars just before the by-pass and that the road was partially closed for a few hours."

"So you're thinking that they would have left the motorway? What route would they have taken then?" Silas enquired.

"Ah, well..." Ferguson shook his head. "Could be a number of off-motorway routes in order to get onto the

R458, the Limerick road. I think that's where he would have made for."

All three were standing now and peering at the area to which Ferguson was pointing. A cluster of small towns and villages with names that meant nothing to them only served to lower their spirits even further.

The office phone rang and Mrs. Peroxide answered, waving to Ferguson to pick up the extension.

"Superintendent Tierney for you."

There wasn't much the detective had to say. The coach and its passengers had not yet been traced. He asked for Silas's number and said he'd be in touch. Also that his colleagues in Shannon were going to dig out CCTV footage which would have been available at the toll stations.

Despondently, they filed out of Ferguson's office, each promising to share any news if and when it was forthcoming.

Silas checked his watch for the umpteenth time. It was now half past one and the absence of his troupe was gnawing at his guts like a peptic ulcer. There was a text from the theatre reporting that the van carrying the scenery and props had arrived but the Arcanum dancers had not shown up for rehearsals. Silas texted back. 'Problem with journey. Will keep you posted.' His mind just could not get around a more detailed explanation at the moment as none existed.

"We should have lunch." Clodagh ordered sensibly. "Then we'll hit the road."

★

CO. CLARE.
1735

He had to admit that the turn out was more spectacular than he could possibly have imagined.

Girls and boys, men and women of all ages, shapes and

sizes crowded the barn as he weaved his way through the farmhouse gate to greet them. Faces weathered and furrowed from a lifetime of outdoor toil and faces that had not yet experienced the ravages of time smiled with undisguised pleasure as they watched him approach.

The long grass made it a difficult walk in his dancing shoes and the brambles from the hedgerow threatened to snag his jacket, but there was no doubting that the welcome he was about to receive was one of near idolatry.

Apart from the families paying sixpence a quarter for his services they had also brought gifts of sustenance. A large table expertly crafted from oak and ash which had been lifted from the house by the farmer and a team of strong helpers was covered with offerings of gratitude. It had been a good summer so the early harvest was bountiful, with sheaves of ripe corn, raffia baskets filled with shiny apples, dark plums, firm potatoes and onions. Barley bread was knitted into spiral shaped loaves, and oatmeal, eggs and mushrooms resided in earthenware pots. Honey comb and fresh garlic were used to fill the few spaces left between jugs of buttermilk and mead and the scent of honeysuckle wafted towards his nostrils along with lavender and musk roses.

A girl of around five or six with hair the colour of mustard seed ran towards him holding out a daisy chain, her chubby cheeks warming as he stooped to receive it and patted her curls. He smiled as she ran shyly towards her beaming mother and buried her face in her apron.

The men drew him towards the table slapping his back in hearty greeting. The women, some of them barefoot, kept their distance but looked on giggling as he took a swig of mead and turned to admire their full skirts and petticoats painstakingly chosen and sewn for the occasion.

A few of them were ripe for bedding he thought wiping his mouth with the back of his hand. One in particular was certainly worthy of his fancy. Kathleen, the wife of the blacksmith Thomas Dooley, her hair as ebony as raven's wings and skin like polished marble placed her hands onto her slim waist in as seductive an invitation to the dance that he could imagine.

Another sup of mead and he wouldn't keep them waiting any longer. Slightly unsteady but also drunk with the power that came with the legacy, he began to form them into lines as the farmer who owned the barn pushed forward a blind fiddler in torn and dirty garments to stand by his side ready to play.

The old ones weren't worth bothering with so he chose only the young men and women and when he had positioned them in the order he had selected, the new Dance Master then cued the fiddler and watched as the small assorted company metamorphosed into a whirling, rhythmic kaleidoscope of pure motion.

They had been tutored well by his silver-haired predecessor and their discipline and control matched their enthusiasm. They held their bodies rigidly, moving only from their hips downwards, their arms flat by their sides until suddenly the fiddler broke into a wild jig and then they clenched and waved their fists to the music in the threatening gesture of opposition to foreign occupation.

From her position on a mossy knoll a few feet from the action, the crone who had served her Master for two decades observed the pageant with intense interest. She scrutinised the amount of mead that had been imbibed and the boy's hand lingering a little too long around Kathleen Dooley's waist. She noticed too his apparent impatience with the older members of the community and a certain arrogance that she had missed when first her Master had made his choice.

Reaching into the folds of her long skirt, the toothless hag took out a precious item wrapped in a velvet pouch and stroked it lovingly. Her Master had told her of his many travels in distant lands before she had given her life to his service. He had visited ancient Egypt where he had become fascinated by the myths and cultures he had encountered there. He had also worked in the courts of northern Italy and talked of that period as Renaissance, translating it for her benefit as 'Rebirth'.

His attention had been captured there by a certain pagan practice of divination which he had embraced wholeheartedly. A map of the imagination which was not merely simple fortune telling.

The woman had learned how to divine the art and considered herself now an expert, although caution had to be exercised for the clergy had long condemned the 'Trionfi' which her Master had gifted her as the ladder to the gates of hell.

Anyway, she preferred to refer to its much simpler name – The Tarot.

★

They can vanish sometimes, the people closest to us. Disappear without trace leaving us bewildered and bereft. You hear about it all the time. Adults, children, even boats and planes.

Clodagh struggled to feel optimistic as the Ford Fiesta purred its way towards Ennis on that late September afternoon. The leaves were already beginning their transition to gold and a bitter-sweet melancholia descended upon the air in a haze of autumn moistness.

Conversation between the three of them was limited. Silas drove with an expression of grim concentration, his eyes occasionally darting left and right when he thought he might have spied a similar type of coach to the one he had hired. The stark truth was that they had not encountered any that looked even remotely like it anywhere on the journey. Stopping to fill up at the motorway service station they had enquired if a vehicle of that description had been there sometime during the early hours, but were rewarded with the shaking of heads, promises to check with colleagues and no, they didn't have CCTV.

Nothing. A negative word that carried so much weight and on hearing Silas say it yet again that weight pressed heavily on Clodagh's heart. She desperately needed to believe that her friends would by now have arrived at the theatre, filling it with their chatter, colour and laughter while they prepared for tonight's show.

Justin was stretched out on the back seat sleeping. How she wished that she could sleep away the events of the last twenty-four hours. First there had been her injury. A silly mistake which should never have happened. Turning on her foot the wrong way during those double clicks had put the production in jeopardy and she found it hard to forgive herself for such carelessness.

Then of course there was the dream. The dream she could not erase from her mind. It seemed to beg to be understood and yet she struggled to grasp its meaning. Why was she giving herself such bewildering advice while dressed as a character in a pack of fortune-teller's cards? How could she use that advice, anyway?

But by far the worst of those events was the one they were all living through now and Clodagh realised that at some point very soon the parents and friends of those missing would wonder why they hadn't received a phone call or a text from their loved ones.

She considered reminding Silas of this but then decided against it. He had enough to think about and it would only add to his anxiety. She thought of her own parents and how they would react to such a strange and unsettling situation. An only child, she had grown up in a comfortable middle-class home doted on by her mother and father and their tight knit closeness had never been threatened.

She hadn't been pressured into studying the Irish dance. In fact, it had been quite the opposite. While the other children of her age were being pushed and cajoled into taking lessons, often to please their mothers' own thwarted and frustrated ambitions, Clodagh had always been ready and willing to learn to perfect what she loved to do. Dressed an hour before leaving for her classes, she would carefully smooth down the short, emerald taffeta skirt which she wore over her black leggings, curl her long red hair and practice her warming-up exercises in the cosy, Aga-centred kitchen of her parents' County Wicklow home.

When she was seven, the family moved to the Dublin suburb of Donnybrook where her father had been offered a lucrative partnership in a leading law firm and it wasn't difficult for her mother to also secure a part time job as a primary school teacher. But the best thing about the move for Clodagh was the proximity to her Auntie Peggy. Her mother's sister lived in Dublin and taught Irish dance at her own prestigious school. A four time Irish champion winner, Peggy never considered herself good enough to go pro. Also, Irish dance was not a very fashionable profession to follow in the eighties. It had lost its bite and many thought it had had its day, but then the whole attitude towards it changed in the mid-nineties when a group called Riverdance burst into people's consciousness and at that precise time her brilliant niece came to live nearby.

Peggy adored having Clodagh in her class. Not just because she was her niece but because she was so very good. "You dance from the heart Clodagh," she used to say. "That is important. The steps have to be right, but, particularly in a set dance it is essential to dance from the heart and immerse yourself in the story."

Entering Clodagh in her first feis when she was twelve was nerve-wracking for the whole family, although Clodagh rose above her nerves and delivered a stunning performance which she was to repeat time and again. Soon she was competing in regional, national and international competitions and travelling all over the world, adding more trophies to her parents' already overflowing cabinets.

In 2009 while competing in a feis in New York she met Silas Murphy. There was no hint of a sexual relationship; Clodagh was then dating a young actor from the Abbey Theatre and Silas had a long-time girlfriend in his home town of Boston. But they clicked immediately, sharing the same dedication and vision for their respective futures and determined to work together as soon as an opportunity presented itself.

Clodagh had never seen a better male dancer since Michael Flatley nor such an imaginative choreographer. Silas told her that his plan was to come and live in Ireland, embrace the culture and eventually form a troupe there. He had a daring and ambitious idea for a set dance which he was starting to put together with an American composer friend and he hoped to make the move sooner rather than later.

Suddenly the harsh sound of a blaring horn jolted her out of her reverie and she was aware of Silas swerving the car to avoid a lorry which had overtaken them, finally screeching to a halt at the edge of a country lane. During her daydreaming the whole landscape had changed from the boring monotony of a concrete roadway to one of rural pastureland, where sheep grazed contentedly beneath mountain ranges, white-washed cottages sat bathed in a salmon sunset and purple-leaved yellow Sorrel sprouted defiantly by the roadside.

"Idiot!" Silas yelled, then turned to Clodagh and Justin. "Everyone alright?"

Clodagh nodded. "Where are we?"

Silas checked the satellite navigation. "I've come off the motorway at one of the exits where Ferguson thought the coach might have done. Now we're going the country route and because I don't want to get to Ennis too late, I'm just going to follow the road signs. The coach driver might have done that if his sat. nav. failed. This is somewhere called "Moneygall.""

"Wait a minute," Justin said, allowing himself a brief smile. "Isn't that where…?"

"Sure it is." Silas nodded. "I thought I knew the name. Obama came here a couple of years back to trace his ancient ancestors."

"It's lovely," murmured Clodagh, winding down her window and enjoying the sound of birdsong striking up an evening chorus.

"Yeah, pity we haven't got time to enjoy it's delights," Silas told them solemnly. "While we've stopped though, I'll try the theatre again."

The others could tell from his conversation that the dancers had still not shown up. The manager, a woman called Deirdre McCall had told him that cancellation notices had been put up and the audience for that night would be having their money re-funded. She was desperate for a meeting and Silas assured her that they were on their way.

They lapsed into silence again as Silas started the car and they continued their cheerless journey through yet more picturesque countryside and coastal roads each hoping and praying that they may find some answers before they arrived in Ennis.

Despite herself, Clodagh fell asleep. And somewhere, just past the magnificent Dromoland Castle Hotel with its rich history and famous patronage, the torn muscle in her calf was inexplicably healed.

★

Forty-nine year old Detective Superintendent Joe Tierney finally had the decision made for him. He was told by the Commissioner to temporarily abandon and delegate the two cases he had been working on for weeks and to concentrate on this missing coach and its passengers.

Was this more important than the jewellery robbery in O'Connell Street or the shooting of a young boy on the outskirts of the city he wondered as his chief left the office? At this stage, he didn't think so, but it was an odd and unusual situation that was obviously now calling for action. On a lighter note, his teenage daughter would never forgive him for not making the effort. Sacha, who at sixteen was besotted with the Irish dance and a proud pupil of Miss Peggy O'Neill's school in Grafton Street. Indeed, Miss O'Neill's own niece Clodagh Trevor was the female lead dancer in Arcanum which he had been dragged to see and reluctantly had to admit it was a grand show.

It was 6.00 p.m and the coach had still not arrived in Ennis as planned. There were no reports of it being involved in an accident and the coach company and the family of the driver were all putting pressure on the Garda to find out what had happened.

Now he was going to have to instigate an intensive search in tandem with the Garda Siochana in the County of Clare as well as with the Missing Persons Bureau and possibly the Criminal Investigation Department and it was set to be a complicated and expensive procedure.

Joe Tierney and his colleagues had worked through the most challenging and toughest of times over the last decade as robbery, drug and fraud offences in the city as well as gun crime had risen sharply. Ireland's people were mourning the extinction of the Celtic Tiger, the euro had sunk to an all-time low and the prosperity that had embraced the whole country for one enchanted moment, disintegrated like the bones of the great Republican leaders.

At least he had managed to buy his modest semi-detached house in Clondarf just at the right time and thank God he did not want or need to sell it now, as that would be one hefty problem he could well do without.

He chided those who said everything had improved and that the Celtic Tiger was about to rise again like the Phoenix, maintaining that caution rather than misplaced optimism was better embraced at the moment. He had applied this philosophy not only to his private life but also to his thirty years in the service of the Garda and it had proved, in his opinion, to be the wisest and most effective stance to maintain.

But now here was a case that was threatening to blow apart the carefully managed budgets and would end up using hours of man-power and resources unless he could find this bloody bus. And it had to be somewhere between here and Ennis, didn't it?

Tierney ran his hand over his course, rust coloured hair and realised it badly needed cutting. Try and find time for that, he told himself dismally. Plans had to be made and just where was he to start?

He stared again at his computer screen where the grainy images of the previous night's CCTV from the toll station was frozen. A hand paying the toll fee stretched out of the driver's side of the coach before the shiny, black vehicle slowly departed for the motorway. Where the hell had it gone from there?

With a sinking feeling he knew there would have to be a public appeal. The families of the people who were missing would expect no less. Then of course there was the press. It wouldn't take long for a story like this to get out and be sensationally reported and for the ripples to spread. The appeal would have to be combined with a press conference and where better to set it up but the theatre in Ennis where he knew the choreographer and Clodagh Trevor were now.

He realised he would have to try and arrange all this for the morning. It would be then over twenty-four hours since the coach had left Dublin and a decent amount of time given up to searching would have already elapsed.

Joe Tierney buckled down to a long night ahead including a drive to Ennis. Mysteries were there to be solved and he was determined not to let this one escape him.

★

Deirdre McCall was a short, no-nonsense woman of indeterminate age with long, mousy hair swept into a doughnut, a penchant for Celtic costume jewellery and billowing flowery tops worn over black trousers. She had worked her way up to Manager of the Irish Music Theatre in Ennis from years of backstage and management experience in various regional theatres around the country, her last senior position being Chief Administrator in the prestigious Gaiety Theatre in Dublin which she left three years ago in order to care for her sick mother in her home county of Clare.

This evening she spoke in a calm and business-like tone making it clear that speculation regarding the whereabouts of the troupe was off the agenda at the moment and that she could not afford to allow the theatre to remain empty for much longer.

Silas said he understood, although he had been hoping for some empathy and understanding of something he was powerless to do anything about. Deirdre softened somewhat after about an hour and as they sat in the plush red seats of the stalls facing the Arcanum scenery that had been set up earlier that afternoon, she voiced her concern.

"What are you going to do, Silas?"

"Honestly, Deirdre, I haven't a clue. Let's see what the cops come up with. At least it's been classified as a missing persons case now and they are actively searching. The worst thing I have to do tonight is contact the families."

His energy depleted, he had asked Justin to take Clodagh and their bags to the hotel. Joe Tierney had called and Deirdre had agreed that an appeal and press conference could take place at 10.00 am at the theatre the following morning. He would need to be on top of that and would try and get a good night's sleep, although that prospect seemed unlikely with the many concerns that were flooding his mind.

"Would you and Clodagh be willing to dance here for me?" Deirdre ventured, studying his worried face. "Until they turn up, I mean?"

Silas was surprised. It was something he would never have considered and wasn't sure how it could happen.

"Well, for a start Clodagh has a leg injury. That's why she didn't leave in the coach as planned. And I haven't choreographed anything for the two of us that doesn't involve the troupe."

"I don't mean to sound insensitive." Deirdre told him. "But if they don't arrive and the press make a meal of this, which I'm sure they will, then the publicity for you and this theatre would be pretty full-on. None of us can do anything that the police aren't already doing, so we have to do something. I'm not suggesting a full show, I can book other acts in, but if we had the two of you dancing together or dancing solo as guest artistes, that might help us all. You don't have to make a decision right now, but please think about it."

Silas stood up and paced along the row of seats his brain in turmoil. How could he even consider working out a routine for himself and Clodagh while his troupe were missing? Or consider working at all? But Deirdre had a point. Although he didn't want to entertain the notion that another day might go by without them being found or God forbid more than another day, he couldn't just sit around waiting and making himself sick with worry.

"Let me sleep on it." He told her and she nodded. "And see what happens tomorrow."

He saw Justin walking in and waved him over. "What happened with the hotel?"

Justin flopped into a chair in the row in front of them. "Awkward. They say they can't hold the rooms past tonight."

Deirdre rose explaining that she had a mound of e-mails to attend to. "I'll see you in the morning. You've got my mobile number if there's any news and don't be afraid to ring at any hour."

Silas allowed himself to be pecked on the cheek as she swept out of the theatre, leaving a trail of Yves St. Laurent's "Opium" wafting in her wake.

"Where's Clodagh?" He asked Justin, who had enviably changed into a clean T-shirt and was wearing a blue sweater fashionably draped around his shoulders.

"At church."

An inappropriate response hovered on the edge of Silas's tongue which he swallowed hastily. 'What's she doing there?' would have been an insane thing to say in the circumstances. He knew how important Clodagh's faith was to her and of course she was there praying for her friends.

"Silas, did you notice she wasn't limping when you dropped us off?"

"No. What are you saying?"

Justin decided to abandon the fashion statement and pulled the sweater on over his head. "Just that. She wasn't showing any sign of her injury. In fact, walking completely normally."

"Did you ask her about it?" Silas was puzzled. "It can't be better yet."

"No, it can't. A tear like that can't suddenly mend itself. And yes, I did ask her and she just said 'It's okay now.'"

"I need her to help me with telling the families. We have to do that tonight before they hear it from the press. Let's go."

There were too many odd things happening which were difficult to explain and Silas had neither the energy nor the inclination to give the matter any further thought when more pressing and immediate practicalities were demanding his attention.

★

It had to be the most agonizing experience of their lives, making those calls to the loved-ones of the missing. The sense of futility when each call ended took them beyond pain.

Each pick-up had begun with the usual greeting. "Silas, how are you?" "Clodagh, how lovely to hear from you," and then the silences, the sheer disbelief and finally the choking sobs and little in the way of goodbyes.

How could either of them offer any comfort when comfort was just a barren space in a distant wilderness?

For a little over two hours Silas and Clodagh sat side by side on a strange bed, each on their respective phones, talking, crying, pulling themselves together and then repeating the procedure. Finally, at nearly midnight and after a couple of stiff whiskies, they bid one another goodnight.

Silas caught Clodagh's wrist as she was leaving his room. "How's your leg? Justin said it was better."

He had never seen her so pale. At that moment she took on the appearance of a waif-like ghost, just a visitor in his concept of reality.

"Yes," was all she said and suddenly she was gone. Down the corridor and into another strange room. Moving perfectly, like a dancer.

★

The first thing that struck him was that this morning's events seemed almost ritualistic. Maybe to his fatigued mind it was because the backdrop consisted of the Arcanum set. The Tower, the Moon, the throne between the pillars, even the now sadly comical cut out of the Hanged Man which had toppled over and been placed lopsidedly against one of the flats.

He hadn't shaved and now regretted it. Particularly as the high priest of stubble, coach company manager Conor Ferguson, was looking as shiny as the proverbial infant's lower cheeks.

Superintendent Joe Tierney had pulled out all the stops and the theatre was filled with journalists from the regional and national papers as well as television and radio represented by RTE, the BBC and Sky. Lap tops and tablets were perched on knees, and mobiles were ever ready for text and twitter action.

As the growing number of voices in the theatre buzzed in his ears, Silas realised it was the only time in his life when he had faced an audience who weren't there to see him dance, and it was an unnerving experience.

The group at the table comprised of Tierney in the centre flanked by Conor Ferguson and Silas on his right and Clodagh plus a Superintendent from the Ennis Gardai, Gerry Doyle, to his left. A large map of the area stood on an easel a little way from the table.

Joe Tierney half read the introductory speech he had prepared, the rest he delivered off the cuff. He started by thanking Deirdre McCall for her loan of the theatre and it was, he surmised, the most plausible place to hold the appeal as Arcanum had been scheduled to appear there this week. He ran through the coach's description and departure, mentioning the CCTV pictures taken at the tolling station as the last known sighting of the vehicle.

When he opened up the room for questions, they came in a rapid crescendo and he had to exercise his position to request that each individual wait their turn.

"What's known about the driver?"

Conor Ferguson shaded his eyes with his hand in order to see where the question had come from and replied that Dennis Ahearne had worked for his company for ten years and had an unblemished record. Not so much as a scratch incurred on any of the vehicles he had driven over that period and he was a family man with two adult children.

"Where are you focusing the search?"

Joe Tierney acknowledged his colleague from Ennis who stood up and moved towards the map using a pointer to show the area between the two towns that were off the motorway.

"We're concentrating our search on the whole area off the M18 en route to Ennis. We know that an accident partly closed the motorway just before the Ennis by-pass at approximately ten past one yesterday morning. The coach, along with other diverted traffic could have gone a number of ways but we believe it would have made for the Limerick Road. It wasn't a tourist, sight-seeing coach and it was dark so there was no need to take the scenic routes, just the quickest one."

"How many dancers on the coach and are they all Irish?"

Tierney nodded to Silas who leaned forward into the microphone. "There's twenty-four dancers and one stage manager. There are three non-Irish dancers among them. One Spanish, one German and one from the U.S. We haven't been able to make contact with any of them on their cells. There were also costumes and music backing tracks on board. Props and scenery were transported separately."

"Has kidnapping been considered?"

Tierney shook his head. "Not at this stage. It seems highly unlikely that anyone would go to the trouble of holding a large coach-full of people to ransom and no-one has been in touch demanding money. However, we're not ruling anything out."

"Are you using the internet as a means of spreading the search?"

"We're mounting a campaign on Twitter and Facebook. Silas and Clodagh will be doing the same from their social media sites. I believe there will be photos of the missing posted on the Arcanum website. Now, if there are no further questions, I will ask Silas Murphy to just say a few closing words."

He had decided that he couldn't write anything down. He also couldn't be bothered to maintain an air of dignity or deliver well-mannered platitudes. The natural stamina that had carried him this far was overtaken by a burst of emotional adrenalin and he found himself standing up in order to project this so aptly named appeal with tears burning in eyes already throbbing from lack of sleep.

If he closed them, strained his senses to evoke it, he could conjure up the vision of his dancers and then he would open his mouth and let the words flow in a torrent towards ears straining to what he had to say. His mouth and lips were stress-dry and he sipped water from a glass, aware that a silence as heavy as a midnight snowfall had descended on the theatre.

"I've watched so many television appeals for missing people. I've looked through the screen into the eyes of mothers, fathers, sons and daughters, husbands and wives. Seen the pain etched on their faces, heard their crying, sensed their bewilderment and helplessness. But I was always an observer, an outsider. I never thought the day would come when I would be making my own desperate appeal for people so close to me they might as well be family.

None of us can understand what has happened. It's not as if it's a small vehicle, it's a bloody great coach with twenty-five people on board plus the driver. Someone – no, many people, must have passed it, noticed it simply because it's not that common a sight on the road.

If any of you out there were on or around the motorway last night or during the last twenty-four hours, I'm appealing

- begging you, if you think you might have seen something that can help us, then please, please come forward with information. Anything at all. Please...."

He heard Clodagh choke back a sob and pressed on, sensing the cameras moving in closer for maximum effect and the frantic activity from the newspaper reporters as they conveyed what he was saying to their computers.

"....Finally, I'd just like to thank Superintendent Tierney and Superintendent Doyle from the Dublin and Clare Gardai for acting so promptly as well as the MPB, and I believe that numbers will be going out at the bottom of the screen now for you to ring with information. Thank you and God bless you."

He sat down heavily and emptied his water glass as Clodagh ran to embrace him. The assembled media shuffled a noisy exit while the two detectives remained on the platform deep in conversation.

Conor Ferguson touched his shoulder. "Well done, laddie. Let's hope we get somethin' from it, eh?"

Silas nodded, feeling spent, but nursing a fresh optimism fuelled by the amount of coverage he was sure this morning would have produced.

"What do we do now?" asked Clodagh, pushing a fistful of damp tissues into her tapestry bag.

"We wait." Silas told her. "Then I suppose we do what we always do. Dance."

★

CO. CLARE.
1735

The peat fire was dying, throwing a burnt orange glow across the small room as the two bodies on the feathered mattress twined and intertwined once again in the art of copulation.

He hadn't taught her anything she didn't know about

dancing but he had taught her everything she didn't know about sex.

Kathleen Dooley had no idea that anyone could make love so fiercely and savagely. When he came inside her for the third, or was it the fourth time, she uttered a piercing, gull-like cry which rose up through the thatched roof where it was carried on the wind towards the fields leading down to the lake.

How could she not compare this young man to her husband in matters of the bedroom? Thomas was neither lithe nor supple. Lumbering upon her he seemed as heavy as one of the horses he shoed and came quicker than a spark from his hammer before falling into a snoring stupor.

It had been considered a good marriage arranged by the matchmaker and approved by both families, provoking some envy from other girls of marrying age in the area. The blacksmith was a well-respected figure and Kathleen had boasted in those early days that many of the rich gentlemen from the surrounding towns and villages would make the journey to his forge, eager to patronize his expertise. The horses and carts trundling home with turf from the bog or loaded with hay from the meadows, going to the creamery with milk in the early morning all contributed to making the smithy a local necessity, aside from Thomas's skills as a toolmaker with flint, iron and other metals.

But for Kathleen the icing had worn thin and she was bored. He had not made her pregnant and she had no desire anymore to share his bed or bear him children. She had also become aware that he had grown more indifferent towards her of late which suited her fine, and that his affections seemed more inclined towards his ugly black dog than for his lusty wife.

But this one was a different kettle of fish. A charmer for sure. She had never seen anyone with eyes that shade of blue and his wide smile showing unusually good teeth were what she had noticed first about him when he sauntered up to the barn on that warm September day.

And he hadn't just taught her about the art of making love. He had persuaded her to become his drinking companion. Young Kathleen Dooley who at twenty-one had only ever supped barley water or warm milk straight from Gilligan's cow, was now enjoying the heady pleasures of elderflower wine and tangy mead and it served to heighten her experience of sex even more.

She reached beside the bed for the stone bottle and raised it to her lips then passed it to him, giggling as the potent liquid drizzled on to her chin and which salaciously he licked away.

Even through the rosy glow of sex and wine, she knew they were late. That the eighty or so locals who had studied under the old man were keen and ready to continue their tuition and would certainly blame her as well as himself for keeping them waiting. The looks they would throw her way would be contemptuous, some filled with loathing, especially from the crone who used to serve him. The old woman always watching, playing with her infernal pack of cards. A nosy and creepy biddy if ever she'd seen one.

Kathleen pulled on her red blouse that had seen better days and roughly wiped away his sperm with her hemp skirt before tying it round her waist. She ran her fingernails like a comb through her long, dark hair and supped again from the bottle. He drew her towards him but she fought him like a she-cat defending her young, surprising and exciting him with her animal energy.

"Is leor sin!" ("Enough!")

The hazy days of August had passed and colder air was whistling in from the north bringing driving rain which battered the windowless mud houses in the poorer parts of the village and drove the cattle and pigs inside to share some meagre warmth with their owners.

She ran to the door flinging a shawl over her head and laughed drunkenly at the relentless weather, hearing him call as she bolted across the grass, running in her lace-up ghillies like a wild deer across the field and towards the footpath that led to the farmer's barn.

The sound of the fiddle echoed towards her in a haunting lilt and her steps became even lighter, barely brushing the ground as she embraced the storm that enveloped her. Now it had become a dizzying, melodic race to join those souls who waited patiently to be guided in their desire for the dance, a desire for physical and spiritual release from decades of penal laws, poverty and the daily restraints of their lives.

But sated from the excesses of that day, the one who was chosen to be their saviour, unmindful of his calling or his destiny slept the dreamless sleep of the infant or the Fool.

★

The following morning, after the live television appeal, many of the nationals as well as the Irish papers, made it their lead story.

Weary of middle-eastern conflicts, fleeing refugees and terrorist atrocities, the press enthusiastically created headlines which read 'This strange story', 'Where did they go?' 'Mysterious disappearance' and it soon became the topic of discussion and debate on chat shows and news programmes across the world as well as on the internet.

Silas and Clodagh, baffled and numbed by the fact that their friends had still not been found, sat bleakly in an RTE studio giving countless interviews to news stations, all-channel breakfast shows as well as contributing to documentaries about the story that were already swinging into production.

By the time they arrived back at the hotel in the early evening, flash bulbs were still popping in their eyes, questions still spinning around in their brains and they knew without doubt that they would have to repeat it all the following day and perhaps beyond.

Nothing tangible had emerged thus far. The appeal had brought a response from a few drivers who had seen the coach in Dublin before it left on the N7. Others had seen it at the toll stations and others at the beginning of the M18.

Lorries and vans, vehicles which were mostly on the road at that late hour, did not report seeing it leave at any of the exits off the motorway.

The Gardai had put notices along the areas which they thought would be the most likely to jog memories and there was a police presence just off some of the main exit routes stopping motorists and showing them photographs of the coach.

Deirdre McCall's theatre was still dark although she had booked in a Gospel choir and a local music group for the following week. Most of the punters had heard about the disappearance of the bus and turned up to get their refunds. A gloomy air of tragedy hung inside the building, touching those who entered with something that they could not define nor wanted to stay around longer to experience.

Justin decided he might as well return to Dublin, particularly as he could do nothing more for Clodagh. He gave her a warm hug and told her to let him know if she needed him.

"Thanks, Justin." Her voice was a little more than a whisper. "I can't explain about my torn muscle. I wish I could."

They were standing in the hotel lobby as people checked in and out, carrying on with the normality that formed the fabric of their daily lives. Many threw curious glances her way as she had now become as familiar and instantly recognisable as the latest reality show celebrity.

She watched Justin leave and then made her way towards the lift, hoping that she could catch an hour's rest before a quiet dinner with Silas and the chance for them to discuss the situation without any other intervention.

"Clodagh?"

She turned quickly to see who had called her name. "Oh, hello Erin."

Erin Shaw was in her early forties. Attractive in a well made-up and structured kind of way, with just the right amount of blonde highlights streaked through her immovable shoulder-length bob, and wearing cherry lip gloss which picked up the primary colour of her Chanel style tweed suit.

"I'm sorry to hear about Arcanum." Her concern held a forced edge. "What a mystery."

"Yes." Clodagh said wearily. "A mystery."

"Clodagh, do you have a minute? I really need to talk to you. Perhaps we could go to the bar?"

"I'm not sure, Erin. I've had a long day and I'm meeting with Silas for dinner."

She wondered why Erin Shaw would need to talk to her. Erin ran an Irish dance company called Lighthouse which had been active on the circuit for about five years and had achieved moderate success in touring up and down the country. She had studied with an old sparring partner of her aunt Peggy's at a school in Drogheda and was an ambitious, forceful and energetic personality.

"Just one quick drink. I won't keep you long."

Curiosity prompted her to accept and she followed Erin to a quiet corner of the hotel bar where the choreographer settled in a high backed chair and ordered a large glass of white wine for herself and a Coke with ice and lemon for Clodagh.

"Clodagh, I won't beat about the bush. I want to offer you the lead female spot in Lighthouse. You would be joining us next month. We've been contracted to a major tour of Australia and New Zealand starting in March next year and the new choreography is awesome. What do you say?"

Clodagh stared at her in astonishment. "But Erin, I have a job as lead dancer with Arcanum."

Erin Shaw took a sip of her Chardonnay then dropped her voice, aware that others in the bar seemed to be taking an interest in their conversation.

"Clodagh, I know that. Of course I do. But they aren't here. What will you do if they aren't found? I can offer you more than Silas pays you and it will take him at least a year to put another troupe together. Please consider it."

"What do you mean, if they aren't found?" Clodagh

couldn't contain her disbelief. "Of course they'll be found. How can you even suggest such a thing?"

Erin leaned towards her addressing her urgently. "At least think about it, Clodagh. Like you, I want to believe they'll be found but you must have given some thought to the possibility that there could have been a tragic accident. You'll need to work. To earn money. It's a good deal, Clodagh."

She drained her glass and stood up, taking a business card out of her pink clutch bag. Placing it on the table in front of Clodagh, she touched her arm gently.

"I'm just a phone call away, but I will need to know by the beginning of November. Ring me."

And she was gone leaving Clodagh feeling even more confused and battered by the rapid onslaught of events than she had been before.

Did Erin have a point? Was it worth considering joining another company when Arcanum's future was hanging in the balance? It was a good offer but how could she abandon Silas now at this crucial time when he desperately needed her support and friendship? More than ever they were connected by a common bond within a maelstrom of emotional uncertainty.

Anyway, Deirdre McCall had suggested that the two of them could headline a season in Ennis. If and when they did decide to dance, then maybe that would be the best option for the short term and they could still be around for their friends when…

Her thoughts trailed into a cloud of miserable despair. And that despair once more threw up the same old questions. Why hadn't they reached their destination? Why couldn't they be contacted? Why hadn't her prayers been answered?

Not wanting to be seen crying yet again, Clodagh rose quickly and made her way out of the bar. She wouldn't need to tell Silas about Erin's offer for there was no way she would be accepting it.

★

The remainder of September and most of October passed slowly and forlornly with the drawing in of damp, foggy nights and the spiteful promise of winter just around the corner. Halloween fireworks and celebrations had begun to excite families up and down the country as grinning pumpkins beamed a candlelight welcome from windows, and in dark shadows figures dressed in sheets and scream-masks hissed and booed and leapt out at unsuspecting night walkers.

For Joe Tierney and his colleagues in Ennis the disappearance of the coach and its passengers had become a nightmare of international proportions as the families of the three non-Irish members of the troupe each from Valencia, Hamburg and Chicago descended on Dublin and County Clare bringing with them a trail of film makers and news teams, lawyers and priests. Each family offered their own reward on their Facebook pages and this in turn attracted the anticipated number of sick prank responses which sent the social network sites almost into meltdown. But there was still an absence of any information that could throw light on the mystery and the Gardai were forced to admit that they were baffled.

Speculation grew, due to this lack of hard information. Twigs of possible news, sightings, rumours were woven into stories. Silas and Clodagh had made the decision to stay in Ennis with Clodagh making the occasional journey home to see her parents. They had taken daily drives in those early days following the disappearance, but the more time passed the more depressing those futile searches had become as they returned each evening with the same dull sense of failure and overwhelming loss.

Silas figured he had nothing to lose by taking up Deirdre's suggestion to work out a programme for the two of them which would certainly draw in the crowds although for all the wrong reasons. They could each perform individual routines and as the Arcanum scenery was at the theatre, he and Clodagh would re choreograph a segment of the Tarot set dance for the two of them. He had copies of the music tapes but they would need to pay for new costumes, an investment which Deirdre was certain they would recoup.

For Silas, having to re-tell the story he had woven from the Major Arcana for his dancers was a painful and difficult process. For the moment he would keep his role as the Diviner, the person who foretells the future through the cards to the Inquirer, who was played by Michael but now would be an unseen character. Without the rest of the troupe to play members of the deck he could only rely on Clodagh's luminous presence as The High Priestess, choreographed as a ballet in an atmosphere of partial silence, before they took the dance to its spirited finale together.

He perched on a stool at the side of the stage, watching her rehearse and marvelling once again on how she had totally absorbed this character. He also found himself reflecting on how it had all started for him and what a great time he had enjoyed before arriving at this present unlikely cross-roads in his life and career.

Born in Boston to an Irish-American family, he was the youngest of four children, of whom the other siblings were girls. His father Patrick was a quiet and thoughtful presence in the home, a master carpenter like his father and grand-father before him, who always managed to put food on his family's table and who loved to read to his children at night which he did until they were around thirteen or fourteen. Silas's mother, like Clodagh's, was a part-time school teacher but also a theatre enthusiast spending many an hour helping backstage with amateur productions of plays and musicals in which the pupils at her school participated.

None of his sisters were in the least interested in Irish dance and when Silas first expressed a desire to learn at the age of seven, they screamed with laughter and teased him mercilessly. Fortunately for Silas, his father and mother encouraged him in his passion, sending him first to a small dancing school for the under twelve's which was situated within walking distance of his home.

After years of suffering bullying at his Catholic preparatory school, being named a faggot and shunned by some of the boys he would have liked to have become friends with, Silas hit the magic age of twelve and then everything he had ever dreamed of was suddenly on the brink of fruition.

An Irish dance group had made a guest appearance in an international European song festival held in Dublin which had been televised it seemed in almost every country in the world, including on a couple of small stations in America. They had actually stolen the show and made headlines in most newspapers the next day.

Soon their fame had reached U.S. shores as the two lead dancers were of Irish-American stock and Silas was shown the video by his excited mother and dance teacher, who managed to record the segment when it was eventually transmitted on ABC.

The young Silas was captivated. Michael Flatley, the charismatic choreographer and lead dancer became his role model and everything he aspired to be. An Irish-American boy who proved that a red-blooded male could make an ancient musical culture into a modern, sexy and exciting form of entertainment.

Silas became obsessed, collecting all the audio and video recordings the dance group had made but the highlight for the young boy was being taken by his parents to see them perform live at the Radio City Music Hall in 1996.

When Flatley left Riverdance and started his own troupe, Silas followed "Lord of the Dance," "Feet of Flame" and "Celtic Tiger" with all the fervour of a religious convert. With the onset of DVDs and the internet, he was able to access as much material as was possible and left the small dancing school he had been attending to study in the bigger and suddenly very popular Boston Academy of Irish Dance.

From then on it was uphill all the way, although he still had to achieve Flatley's unbelievable record of thirty-five clicks a second. Moving from competition to competition, he continued to learn and perform with thoughts and ideas ever crowding his mind on how he could create his own productions which would be seen by audiences all over the world.

Then he met Clodagh. And that memory jolted him swiftly back to the present as he realised she had finished dancing and was looking enquiringly at him for approval.

"Yes. Yes," he shouted and she looked startled. "You've got it. Absolutely."

She was surprised. She didn't think she had got it at all. In fact she was deeply sceptical that the dance could work in this reduced format. The other thing which was bothering her, and she wouldn't tell Silas, was the way the costume was making her feel. Before, she had simply thought of it as another prop necessary for her performance. Something to be worn, taken off and hung up in her dressing-room, then forgotten about until the next time she needed to wear it. Now, something indefinable had occurred, in that the dress itself felt like a second skin. Almost part of her own body and when she removed it she felt naked and exposed.

She wondered a little for her sanity. She could hear Silas speaking to her but wasn't taking in his words. Had this whole unhappy event unhinged her? She suddenly felt a cold wave of fear and needed to get out of the theatre, into the air where she could feel normal again.

He moved forward asking if she was okay and she nodded, stumbling past him anxious to get out of the blue dress and into her jeans and trainers.

Concerned, Silas stared after her. He wished that she would confide in him for he knew that something other than the disappearance of her friends was playing on her mind.

He attempted a humourless soft shoe jig on the dusty stage and heard a door creak open at the top of the auditorium throwing a pillar of light on to the crimson velvet seats.

"Silas!" Deirdre McCall's voice was strange. Higher than usual with an imperceptible hint of hysteria.

"Deirdre? Are you alright?" He jumped down from the

stage and started walking towards her as she ran up the aisle shouting the words that almost stopped his heart.

"Silas, they've found him. They've found the driver."

★

CO. CLARE.
1735

The two handsome horses pulling the elegant black coach came to a halt outside the big house, flaring their nostrils and stamping their hooves, clearly relieved that the two hour journey they had just endured along the rutted country roads was finally over.

He stepped out in full costume, then as the coach drove away and before making his way to the great front door, peered into one of the brightly lit windows, drawing a deep breath and assimilating the scene inside, as perfect and idyllic a picture as he could only have fantasised about until tonight.

Tall candles burned brightly in silver holders on polished tables, flowers that he could have sworn were out of season seemed to bloom in ornate vases as he watched them, a large bowl containing fruit, another filled with walnuts sat on smaller tables beside massive fireside chairs and the tableau was completed by the characters who inhabited it and whom he was about to meet.

Hired by the master of the house to tutor his ten year old daughter and twelve year old son in the minuet and the hornpipe, he was to be paid one gold coin as well as supplied with a free supper courtesy of the housekeeper when the lesson was over.

When he was shown into the drawing room, flanked by two excited wolfhounds, he removed his feathered hat with a flourish and bent into an exaggerated bow which drew giggles from the children who were then gently reprimanded by their mother.

The master of the house was tall and of swarthy appearance, dressed in an embroidered silk waistcoat and grey silk breeches. He carried a riding crop certainly just for effect and bore an air of wealth and power which he appeared to exercise over family and servants alike. His son, although golden-haired, was a minute version of the master, dressed similarly, but wearing buckled shoes for dancing rather than tall leather riding boots.

The women present could have been created from an artist's palette. The pastel coloured silks of their dresses blended delicately against the heavy maroon and cream drapes and damask wall coverings and rustled seductively when they moved.

The lady of the house and mother of the children, had a plain but pleasant face with light brown hair woven into circular braids flattened over her ears. Her beautiful dress was a design of lemon, parsley green and white and she kept her eyes lowered as she daintily worked on needlepoint while seated beside the area where the dance lesson was to take place.

The other woman was playing the harp and she would have been the one he would have bedded that night if he only had the chance. Dressed in lavender silk, her hair flowed long and red over her shoulders and her creamy breasts rose and fell in rhythm with the plucking of her instrument while she purposely kept her eyes very firmly away from his.

He offered the little girl his hand and bowed again to which she replied with a curtsy. Also fair like her brother, her hair was fashioned into bobbing ringlets and the pastel of her dress was a musky rose which accentuated her pink and ivory complexion.

They already had the deportment and carriage of the aristocracy and that made it so much easier. So very different to those peasants in the village, half of whom could not stand straight and who were unable to tell their left from right so that the only way he could teach them was to tie straw around their right ankles making it easier for them to differentiate and understand his commands.

The oriental rug had been pulled back revealing the floorboards on which the dance was to take place. He took a piece of chalk from his pocket and marked a large letter Z on the floor then guided the children by their shoulders into the centre of the floor where he placed them either end of the chalk mark.

Their mother laid aside her needlework and made her way to a delicately carved harpsichord where she sat down and opened the sheet music for the minuet. When she and the harpist received their cue they began to play the melody and he moved the children in a slow dance along the chalk mark, passing each other and finishing in the other's place. They repeated this graceful movement several times before he ordered the boy to approach his sister, bow and escort her back to their starting position where they both bowed to their delighted father.

Dismissing the two women from their musical duties, he then brought out his penny whistle and blew a jaunty tune to which, using intricate footwork, he began to dance the hornpipe, indicating that the children follow him as best they could. When they collapsed with laughter, he gave a mock frown and showed them how to put the accents on the first and third beat of the music and use a rocking motion with their ankles.

When they finally mastered the rudiments of the dance, he blew out another lively tune and their parents rose to applaud the excellent efforts their offspring had achieved.

Later, with a gold coin in his pocket and his belly full of rabbit stew and mead, he bid the servants goodnight in the flagstone kitchen but then remembered he had stupidly left his hat on a chair in the drawing room.

Creeping back up the stairs into the house, he opened the door quietly and seeing no one there, went inside to retrieve the hat while suddenly becoming conscious of a scratching sound emitting from behind a lacquered Chinese screen at the far end of the room. Most of the candles had gone out but there were still one or two flickering on the mantelpiece of the huge stone fireplace and he stopped, rigidly still, wondering whether to advance or to leave. Then he heard something which he recognised all too well as a man and a woman reaching a sexual climax.

Tiptoeing towards his hat with fingers outstretched, he noticed a riding boot protrude from behind the screen together with a brief flash of lavender silk and when he had snatched this most important element of his craft, he let himself quickly out of the house wearing a smirk of satisfaction.

As the coach took him home, he lay back against the leather head-rest and closed his eyes. He would be there again because they were pleased with the way he had tutored the children but it was always useful to have a secret weapon. Just in case.

*

Joe Tierney took the call from Gerry Doyle at precisely ten past ten when he had just added a heap teaspoonful of white sugar to his third milky coffee of the morning. An action of habit and one which he should have surrendered upon recently hearing on the news how this seemingly innocent part of his daily ritual now appeared to have become the most deadly toxin since Hemlock.

Up until then he had started the day in a way that had become routine since the disappearance, checking, double-checking and making calls, no matter how nebulous a particular line of enquiry might seem.

His colleague from Clare told him that Dennis Ahearne had been taken to a hospital in Newmarket-on-Fergus, a town thirteen kilometres from Ennis, after being found by two men fishing earlier that morning at Lake Rosroe, a National Heritage area just north of the town.

Tierney immediately placed a call to the driver's wife who was now setting off for the hospital with her son, but he felt worse than useless and unable to offer any information when she begged to know what had happened. Doyle had told him that the man had seemed confused and disorientated, mumbling incoherently and obviously in some state of shock. His clothes were now being examined by forensics and a new search centred on that particular area had been ordered, complete with sniffer dogs.

He pulled out two aspirin from his desk drawer and swallowed them quickly with his coffee which by now was tepid and unappealing. The pressure over the last two months had been immense with no sign of a breakthrough, but perhaps at last there was some glimmer of light at the end of the Shunnel. He smiled weakly at his stupid play on words and grimaced at the amount of paper work that once again had to be abandoned because of this case.

He knew that Doyle and the County Clare Garda were going to be more stressed than he was by this new development. The driver, although a Dubliner, had re-appeared in that county and all resources would be concentrated on finding the others in the vicinity of the lake. It was also possible that because it was a Heritage site area, this could throw up further complications for Doyle who might want to instigate a dig there. In addition the Parks and Wildlife Service might also feel they should be involved. 'Well,' he found himself thinking, uncharacteristically selfishly. 'That's his problem, not mine.'

But Tierney's problems were still questions crying out for clarification. Where had Dennis Ahearne been during the last six weeks, where was the vehicle and more to the point where were those young people? He knew he would have to arrange another press conference, this time just with himself and Doyle, as the two elderly fishermen had already been giving interviews and yet again the story was poised to continue it's worldwide obsessive trail. He had told Doyle that he would get to Newmarket on Fergus as soon as possible to try and interview Ahearne, but the Clare detective had led him to believe that it wasn't an option at the moment as the man had been heavily sedated.

47

He made more calls. Conor Ferguson from the coach company was keen to go straight to the hospital and was very firmly instructed not to do so. He tried to contact Silas but the phone went to voice mail so he rang Deirdre McCall who told him that Silas and Clodagh were rehearsing in the theatre and that she would pass on the message. Tierney told her that he did not want anyone turning up at the hospital and they would be sent away if they did. He also asked if he could borrow the theatre after the evening performance for a brief press conference that night to which she agreed.

He tried to remember when he was last in the area where Ahearne had been found and realised that it was about four years ago when he had taken the family for a trip to the ancient prehistoric walled village of Mooghaun. They had walked up to the fort, the largest and oldest in Ireland, through a delightful pathway shaded by tall oak trees and filled with wild flowers and looked down upon stunning countryside dotted with glimmering lakes and the panoramic view of the Shannon and its estuary stretching into the distance.

He recalled thinking that there had been a very unusual feel to the place and he experienced a kind of dislocation which he put down to mild vertigo, for Joe Tierney was not the sort of man given to flights of fancy or who harboured the remotest belief in the supernatural. In fact, he was still incredibly proud of his last annual report which stated that although he was someone who worked on his instincts, his strength was his ability to maintain a cool and logical head, solving cases as one would a mathematical equation, with diligence and perseverance.

It was strange though, reflecting on that walking trip now and the sensations it evoked. He wondered whether his wife and children had experienced anything similar but would never have mentioned it to them at the time fearing the embarrassment of their taunts and teases.

He concluded that no-one should be surprised at anything in this country, after all, Ireland, the land of the Celtic Twilight, was seeped in superstition and historic folk-lore and where even in the twenty-first century a wide population still believed in the little people and the Banshee screeching out the coming of death. And sure, didn't they even hold up the extension of the motorway from Limerick to Galway for ten years to protect the so-called 'Faery Tree?'

But it would be probably be best to keep thoughts like these to himself. For now.

★

Deirdre, Silas and Clodagh sat zombie-like in front of the rolling news network where the coverage about the driver being found was played and re-played.

The more verbose of the two men who had discovered him was clearly enjoying his moment in the spotlight, in fact it was obvious that he had never been this excited since catching his first trout in the lake in 1969. His parboiled red complexion deepened with each sentence he uttered and he did not falter from his carefully prepared script.

"I taught it was a tinker because he looked very rough. Very rough indeed. He came running…"

"No, it was more stumbling…" Interrupted his less vocal companion.

"Sure, stumbling towards us, shouting and panting he was until he fell down. Just in front of us, just like that. Fell down"

"What was he shouting?" Enquired the interviewer.

"Couldn't make no sense of it." Replied parboiled. "Talking in riddles."

"Aye, in riddles." Echoed his companion.

"Did he say where the others were?"

"Nuttin. Nuttin about dem. Nuttin at all."

Deirdre reached for the remote and clicked the television into silence. They had all heard and seen enough and still none of it made sense. Silas and Clodagh's phones tinkled with incoming texts from friends and families of the missing

49

and they found themselves responding once again with 'We know no more than you do.'

Deirdre opened a small fridge and took out a bottle of white wine. It was nearly lunchtime and she felt they'd earned a drink. As she distributed it into three plastic tumblers, she raised hers and announced in a strong voice that disguised her doubts. "To finding Arcanum. Today."

"To finding Arcanum." The two dancers repeated with forced cheer.

"Today!" said Clodagh. "They must be found today."

Silas then voiced his decision. "I'm going to the hospital, Clodagh. Are you coming?"

Deirdre frowned. "You won't be let in. Tierney said no-one would be allowed in. And good luck in trying to get past the press pack."

"I can't just sit around doing nothing. Let's go, Clodagh."

She hesitated, wanting so much to get to see the driver. To scream the questions at him which were choking her with their tyranny. They would certainly be told they couldn't enter his room but she visualised a familiar film script scenario where she would burst in through a barrage of security guards and white-uniformed hospital staff, rush to his bedside tearing away any tubes that were attached to his body and shaking him fiercely in order to get him to tell her where the others were.

"Okay." She said, picking up her bag. He was right about doing something, even if that something turned out to be a waste of time.

Deirdre followed them through to the front doors of the theatre. "I understand, I really do, but I don't want you to get into trouble."

Silas embraced her in a bear hug. "Thanks, but we'll be fine. See you tonight."

The car journey took only twenty minutes and the dark clouds of evening were already edging in as they approached the hospital. Even if they had tried to get into the car park it would have been impossible as the press were everywhere and men in glowing yellow jackets were trying to keep order and making sure that ambulances and emergency vehicles could park near the entrances.

They left the car a short distance away and realised that Deirdre had been correct in her assumption. They wouldn't be allowed anywhere near the entrance unless they could come up with a foolproof idea.

"Pretend to limp." Silas said suddenly and Clodagh looked at him in surprise. "Pretend you've got your injury back and start limping. You can hold on to me and if we can get into A & E, we'll try and find our way to the ward where he is."

Clodagh smiled at the conspiracy they were about to weave then realised she could improve on the idea. "I've still got the paperwork somewhere from the hospital in Dublin." She rummaged in her bag and produced some crumpled forms. "Here it is!"

"Good girl." Silas was excited now but would not begin to count his chickens just yet. It was possible that the press had tried the same trick and that patients would be very carefully scrutinised before entering the building.

He studied the crowded mayhem that surrounded the hospital and winked at Clodagh.

"Showtime!" He told her and she obediently followed his lead, hopping on one leg and leaning against him for support. Like a pair of drunken crabs they navigated their way towards the A & E entrance and immediately were detained by one of the high-vis. clad security men.

"My girlfriend's injured." Silas lied with urgency. "Please let us through."

"I've got to search you." The man looked at them wearily, as though he wished he could be anywhere else but where he was at that moment. "Orders."

Clodagh leaned against the wall and Silas raised his arms. "Go ahead. I'm not a criminal and I'm not press although it's hard to tell the difference these days."

The man grunted and gave him a quick body search. He seemed satisfied then turned his attention to Clodagh.

"Alright, miss. Can I see inside your bag?"

"Of course." Clodagh replied sweetly, thrusting her old patchwork faithful into his hands. "You'll see there's paperwork in there from the National Orthopoedic Hospital in Dublin from a few months back."

He glanced briefly at the forms, scanned their faces once again and then waved them through the revolving glass doors into the accident and emergency unit, where they took their places on a couple of the small chairs that lined a wall surrounded by a wave of humans in various states of discomfort.

"We made it." Silas whispered as he glanced around apprehensively, expecting to be unmasked as the pretender he had become at any minute.

"What now?" Clodagh asked him, almost wishing that she did still have her torn muscle so that they could be believed if challenged.

"If no-one approaches us for our names, and frankly they are so busy I think that's unlikely, then we try and get to the elevators and take it from there."

"But we don't know which part of the hospital he's in without asking."

"Then we'll try every floor." Silas told her determinedly. "There's bound to be loads of security so we'll look out for it."

Holding on to him once again, Clodagh limped towards the lifts as Silas swiftly read the guide to the various floors. Before he could digest the information and press the relevant button, a female voice called out from behind them and they immediately froze.

"Excuse me? Hello there."

They turned to see a vision in white. One of the nursing Sisters of Mercy who threw them a look that demanded obedience.

Feeling cornered and chastised, they spoke together. "Hello Sister."

Silas stepped forward to offer his hand which was refused. "I'm Silas Murphy and this is...."

"I know who you are." The Sister said, sternly but not unkindly. "And I also know why you are here."

"Sister, we are so desperate to know what's happened to our friends." Clodagh pleaded. "I know we shouldn't be here, but do please try and understand."

The nun gave a sigh and softened her expression. "I do, dear. Really I do. But even if I let you wander around the hospital looking for the poor driver, you wouldn't find him because he isn't here."

Silas and Clodagh exchanged puzzled glances.

"How is that?" Asked Silas. "The Gardai told the news people. That's why they're outside."

"I know, dear." The Sister looked around, then drew them away from the busy lifts and over to a quieter corner at the end of the corridor. "But that was just a ploy, a ruse. Is that what they call it?"

"Yes, Sister." Said Clodagh, thinking for one insane moment that she was five and back at school. "But we still don't understand."

"I really shouldn't be telling you this." The Sister's voice dropped to an intimate whisper. "But the poor man is in the psychiatric unit. That's not in this building, it's further up the road and not obviously signed. If you want to try your luck, then by all means do. But I fear it will be impossible."

Silas squeezed Clodagh's hand, knowing that the odds were stacked against them and they would have to abandon their carefully crafted plan.

The Sister nodded, aware of their decision, and fingering her crucifix startled them with her next question.

"How do you feel about not having gone on the coach that fateful evening?"

Clodagh answered quickly. "By the grace of God, Sister, we were spared."

The nun stared at Clodagh for what seemed far longer than the few seconds it took to make her next remark.

"My dear, has anyone ever told you that you are special?"

Silas looked confused as an embarrassed Clodagh

stuttered a response, trying not to think about her dream or what it might have meant.

"Aren't we all special Sister?"

The woman whose calling had been to give her life to God and to others less fortunate smiled. She had looked into this young girl's olive-green eyes and fancied she recognised a highly evolved soul with an undeniable inner wisdom of which the dancer was not yet aware.

"Of course, my dear. But some are chosen."

★

Having been highlighted on the international map for the past two months, the area around Ennis and the surrounding towns and villages was now approaching chaotic. Hotels and B and B's that would normally have been in a state of suspended off-season animation were sending out for more beds to cope with the demand while the pubs and restaurants were heaving with travellers from all over the world, either directly or indirectly concerned with the disappearance.

Silas and Clodagh were due to open their show the following week but had decided with Deirdre that because of the stress they were experiencing they were only really prepared to perform for the second half. Nonetheless, it was already a sell-out with everyone wanting to see Arcanum's famous lead dancers who hadn't taken the mystery bus.

The pair were not exactly thrilled when Deirdre announced that the dance troupe Lighthouse would be opening for them, but had little choice in the matter. Someone had to do it and Silas could see where Deirdre was coming from in hiring Irish dancers. It added to the sense of drama for the audience and appropriately set the scene for their appearance in a more forlorn rendition of their Tarot dance which was to follow.

Clodagh had too much on her mind to worry about Erin flitting around being chatty and irritating. Or that she would once again try to persuade her to join the troupe.

The Sister of Mercy's words yesterday were as cryptic as the High Priestess of her dream. If there was a message out there then she hadn't got it yet and that, coupled with the grief for her friends, only served to make dancing her escape from such undeniably complex issues.

If the driver was talking, then no-one had been told. Neither Joe Tierney nor his colleague in Ennis was communicating with Silas or the press and the searches near the lake and surrounding countryside had so far proved futile.

When they finished rehearsal that day, Silas told Clodagh that he was once again going to try and see the driver even if there was a police presence.

"Superintendent Tierney or the other detective has got to be there." He told her. "They have to see us. Tell us what's happening."

"Silas, the Gardai don't have to do anything they don't want to." She said, concerned by this new hyperactivity that was consuming his personality. "We'll know when they have something to tell us."

"How can you just sit around?" He didn't want to raise his voice but was frustrated by her passivity. "The world and his wife are out there trying to find out what's happened and we are the ones, along with the families, who have the most right to know."

"Okay, Silas. I'll come with you, but I don't think it's going to work."

The Sister had told them that the building was not obvious as a unit connected to the hospital, but from her description they knew they were at the right place and as they drove slowly by, noticed a small sign-post indicating confirmation a few metres from the front door. Amazingly the press had not cottoned on and were still camped outside the main building further up the road.

As he had done before, Silas parked the car five minutes away in a residential area and they walked together in silence down a short hill preparing once again to lie and to beg, anything to try and get nearer to the truth.

A couple were crossing the road on to the pavement towards them and as they came closer suddenly stopped and stared with what seemed like more than just simple curiosity. The woman was tall, around fifty, with a pinched white face and wearing a leather coat, her badly permed hair blown into a fuzzy helmet by the November wind while the younger man was also tall wearing a trench style raincoat and tweed cap. Silas felt he knew him but couldn't place where they might have met.

The woman spoke as Silas and Clodagh hurried on, now all too familiar with people gaping or trying to engage them in conversation.

"Are you the dancers?"

Groaning inwardly, Silas stopped, feeling that he couldn't just ignore the question.

"Yes. Hello."

To his alarm, the woman grabbed his hand pulling him close and crying pitifully. "Save him. You've got to save him."

Her companion tried to coax her away. "Come on now ma. Don't be worrying the man."

Silas then realised he must be the coach driver's son. The narrow eyes and blotchy complexion were now quite recognisable in a face drawn with grief.

"Are you Mrs. Ahearne?"

Brushing away tears with her coat sleeve she nodded as Clodagh placed a comforting arm around her shoulders.

"How is your husband?" Clodagh asked gently.

Mrs. Ahearne attempted to pull herself together as Silas, spotting a wooden bench on the pavement a little further down the hill, led them to it, indicating that they all sit and talk.

"He's bad. Not himself at all. The doctors say he has some psychotic disorder probably resulting from alcohol dependence when he was younger. Yes, he drank but he's been dry for years. They keep asking me about depression or dementia and I keep telling them he's never had nothing like that since we've been married."

"Has he said anything about what happened?" Silas pressed.

"Nothing that makes any sense, but the hospital say he's suffering from hallucinations so he's got to have something called a PET scan to look at his brain. They think it might be schizophrenia. They're giving him vitamins and have tested him for drugs which proved negative."

"What has he said though?" Silas struggled to keep his patience while maintaining a degree of understanding.

The woman spoke between sobs. "He keeps saying 'They've got 'em, they've got 'em.' But not who the 'they' are. The detectives say it looks like abduction or kidnapping. But I said 'wouldn't someone have come forward and demanded a ransom by now?' It's all crazy and he's not getting any better and he'll be taking all the blame. That's why I'm wondering if you…" She broke off and grasped Clodagh's hand. "If you two would try and talk to him. Maybe it would jog his memory. Please…"

There was nothing that Clodagh and Silas would have liked better and this encounter had lit a beacon of hope in that the driver's wife was actually begging them to visit her husband. However, they knew they would have to get permission from the Gardai and that might prove a far more difficult task.

Silas explained this gently and the woman pulled out a mobile phone from her imitation Louis Vuitton handbag.

"I know one of them is there now. The Dublin one." She told them. "We've just left and he was there. I've got both their numbers."

"Would his phone be switched on?" Clodagh asked. "Sometimes in hospitals they don't allow it."

Mrs. Ahearne shook her head. "No, his is definitely on. I saw him taking calls and reading texts just this morning in my husband's room."

She dialled a number while they all waited expectantly for the call to be answered.

Joe Tierney told them categorically that they would only be allowed in if they told no-one about the locale or about any conversation that might pass between them and Dennis Ahearne. If they did so, he said, he would be unwilling to share any future information with them.

Silas and Clodagh readily agreed and along with Mrs. Ahearne and her son were shown into the small private room where the driver had been admitted. Joe Tierney had arranged for more chairs and there was very little space for manoeuvre.

They had scant idea of what to expect but the shock far exceeded what they might only have imagined.

The man in the bed did not in any way resemble the driver whom Silas had met on the night the coach left Dublin.

The purple mottled complexion had given way to fish-belly white and in a macabre sense it was like looking at a reanimated corpse. His cheeks were hollows under jutting cheekbones and the eyes sunken, creating the illusion of his flesh having begun to decompose from his skull.

While Silas and Clodagh struggled to keep their composure, a hospital orderly slid into the room and retrieved a tray containing a soup bowl and plate of half eaten food. He shot a curious look at the group before leaving as quietly as he had entered allowing Silas to wonder nervously if the staff at the hospital had literally been sworn to silence.

Dennis Ahearne's eyes were the most chilling thing about him. They were not dead eyes but those of someone who appeared to have gone over the edge into madness.

His wife was trembling, holding on to her son's arm, while Joe Tierney maintained an impassive expression despite obviously finding the chair he had been sitting on for hours deeply uncomfortable.

"Do you want to ask him anything?" The Superintendent suggested to Silas and Clodagh before they took their seats.

"Okay." Silas cleared his throat and they approached the

bed, carefully trying to draw answers from the patient but without success.

"Dennis, Silas here. Do you remember anything about the people you say have got my troupe?"

"Dennis, it's Clodagh Trevor. Can you remember what happened to the coach? And to our friends?"

With the minutes passing and nothing forthcoming, Joe Tierney beckoned Silas to join him in the corridor.

"We're no further forward." He told him. "He keeps repeating that someone has got them so we have to look at abduction. His clothes have come back from forensics and simply show grass and mud deposits from around the area where he was found. There were no clues in his pockets either, just some euros, a half packet of fags, a lighter and his mobile phone which hadn't been used since the day he left. "

Silas thought he was tilting at windmills and told him so.

Joe shook his head. "I hear what you're saying, but in the absence of any other information that is the direction we have to take. They're still doing tests here and we hope that we can extract more from him in the days to come. But as you see, he's pretty far gone."

"You've read what the world seems to be implying on the internet?"

The detective gave a half smile. "What, that it's something paranormal? That they've disappeared like those planes in the Bermuda Triangle? Yes, I've seen it and obviously dismissed it as baloney."

Silas shrugged. "Okay. I'm not saying I believe it, but we aren't left with many other options unless someone comes out of the woodwork making demands for their release. And incidentally, if you look closely at the net you'll see there are far more unexplained disappearances than something that happened fifty years ago."

"And you and I both know how many weirdos are out there in Cyberland."

Their conversation was then abruptly halted by a scream and the two men sped back into the room assuming it must be Clodagh. But it was Mrs. Ahearne who had screamed while Clodagh stood silent and calm, locked to the corpse-like figure in the bed.

Silas rushed towards her instinctively.

"Stay away." Dennis Ahearne was clearly terrified but kept his impossibly tight grip on Clodagh's wrist. "Don't come any closer. Stay away."

"Dennis." His wife pleaded. "Let her go, Dennis. Please?"

"What do they want, Dennis?" Joe Tierney raised his voice authoritatively in order to be heard above the din. "What do the people who have the dancers want?"

Dennis Ahearne's eyes rolled in his head and with a supreme effort somehow they managed to locate Silas. Releasing Clodagh's hand he forced out a diabolic cackle causing each of them to feel their blood freeze.

"You, Silas Murphy. They want you!"

★

COUNTY CLARE.
1735

Mick Gilligan, the farmer, was an uneducated man but he considered he had much in the way of what was called common sense and little time for sentiment. Now, even he had to admit there were fewer sadder sights than those which filled his musty barn on that damp September afternoon.

A long brown rat scuttled across his boot and he observed it without rancour. Normally he would grab the broom and try to beat it into another world but today, if he could, he would have used that same broom on a far more noxious animal. One with red-gold curls and a purple feathered hat.

The fiddler was scratching out a jig but the mood was anything but joyful. Children in dirty and tattered clothes squabbled as they tried to form themselves into some kind of orderly lines. The older children attempted to guide them

60

and then lost patience, hissing their scorn and contempt before turning their backs and creating their own division of ragged movement.

A sprinkling of adult couples joined hands in an improvisation which bore no resemblance to the tempo of the music and the few good ones who still turned up in the hope of becoming better pushed the less competent out of the way, their faces carved into masks of frustrated determination.

None but the oxen had toiled as long and hard as Gilligan to make his farm fertile and productive. He, like his father and grandfather before him, had foresworn his Roman Catholic faith in order that his son would inherit his life's work, for only the conversion to Protestantism would ensure the passing on to any heirs. But the Protestant ascendency meant also the ascendency of the English gentry, and much Catholic land as well as the best posts in the Church or in high-ranking office was given to newcomers from the other side of the Irish sea thus creating a rich-poor divide that the fortunate few like himself were powerless to revolutionize.

And now it had come to this and Gilligan's blood raced with a fire that seemed impossible to quell. He was bewildered by the speed at which this terrible deterioration in dignity, ability and hope had vanished. Why and how? It was as though he could reach out and touch these people's innocent needs, for this desire to communicate through something primeval had been started here and he was not prepared just to stand by and watch it evaporate.

A sound, barely audible, though loud enough to distract him floated down with wisps of golden straw from the loft above and he looked up in surprise to see not the anticipated rodent but the sorceress who had served the past Master. Squatting on a pile of sacks with her eyes closed, her lips were moving silently as she consulted the pack of cards that never left her side. He knew from others that she could speak although in all these years he had not heard her and it crossed his mind that she might be trying to communicate with the man to whom she had given so much of her life. But she was not his immediate concern. Instead he re-directed his gaze to the motley gathering before him and knew he would have to take action today.

He believed the rumours to be true. That the boy was spending time giving lessons up at the big house and that he was also fucking Kathleen Dooley. He wasn't sure which made him more angry as Thomas Dooley was an old friend, their families had shared and suffered years of toil and deprivation and he had attended the wedding which had been a merry affair filled with the promise of future blissful harmony.

If Dooley didn't know that his wife was cuckolding him then he was the only one in the village that didn't. Gilligan made the difficult decision to speak to him. He would take his old farm horse there to be shoed and try and engage the blacksmith in conversation about his *scubaide* of a wife in the hope that he could persuade her to be less generous with her favours.

Guiding his grey cart-horse towards the long, narrow white-washed cottage which housed the blacksmith's forge, he found the place quiet and seemingly deserted apart from Dooley's shaggy black dog who began to bark wildly as they came to a stop at the water trough in front of the house.

While his horse enjoyed refreshment, Gilligan patted the dog wondering whether its erect triangular ears and anxious eyes were trying to convey some sort of message. He spoke to the dog reassuringly then walked towards the forge to look for his friend.

Pushing open the heavy oak door, he peered into the darkness where only the last smouldering embers from the furnace offered enough light for him to see there was nobody inside and once again the pungent aroma of sweat, grease and burnt hoof hit him as it always did when he made these visits to Dooley's place of work.

The tools of his friend's trade were a credit to his mastery. The leather bellows were stacked against the furnace next to a table creaking under a variety of tongs, hammers, anvils and horseshoes with only a suggestion of rust visible on any. Axes and chisels lined the old brick walls and row upon row of shiny hooks used for hanging many a copper cooking pot and kettle dangled from the huge cast-iron roof supports, then, caught by a unexpected draught that whistled through the door, rippled together in a peal of percussive harmony.

He could hear the dog barking again and thought that maybe Thomas had returned or perhaps a customer had arrived requiring his services but when he stepped outside into the pale sunshine of the late afternoon, Gilligan found the cobblestone courtyard and the house still deserted.

He decided to allow himself one last look around before returning to the farm and made his way to the back of the house stepping through the nettle-high yard where large well-worn sheets were flapping on the line obscuring the view of the fields beyond.

The dog was at his heels and its intense barking had now changed to a plaintive lament which struck such unease into his heart that he stopped dead in his tracks, squinting into the dappled light which danced on the leaves of the ancient oak tree ahead and whose towering arms seemed to beckon him forward.

And then the sight that Mick Gilligan would carry with him to the grave. That diligent and most upstanding of men, his friend Thomas Dooley, hung by a rope from one of the giant branches, his neck broken and his tongue protruding from an open mouth. A ladder was placed against the tree and beneath it now lay his faithful dog who continued to howl mournfully.

Gilligan rushed towards the tree, looking desperately around for a knife or anything that could cut the rope but it was too late to save the man he had known since childhood. What would drive someone of such conscience and character to commit this final and terrible act? A man as sturdy as the very tree he had chosen to assist him in his death. Burning sorrow rose from the pit of Gilligan's stomach and his spirit felt as bleak as the barren landscape of the Burren. A flock of crows overhead rasped their journey homeward, an eerie and desolate cacophony that did nothing to diffuse the grim horror of his discovery.

Dooley was dead and Gilligan found himself in a wounded place. A place where events seemed to be spinning out of control. He had come here today to try and discover why such sorrow had visited their village and now misery had heaped upon misery.

Maybe there was one person who could give him answers. If he could only get her to talk.

★

The morning after their traumatic encounter with the coach driver, the day dawned fresh and clear and they each woke wishing their minds might enjoy a similar clarity. It was a Saturday and the weekend before the opening of their show, a time when they would normally have spent rehearsing and brushing up on last minute imperfections.

Instead they had decided to join the local community in another search organised by Gerry Doyle and his Clare force together with neighbourhood watch groups from Ennis and Newmarket-on-Fergus. This time the hunt would spread out beyond the lake to other surrounding areas hitherto unexplored and which the willing band of enthusiastic locals was determined to attack with all the energy they could muster.

Clodagh was aware of Silas experiencing some sort of temporary derailment, for it manifested itself in his laughing off the events of the night before. After the initial shock of Dennis Ahearne's outburst he had put it down to the ramblings of a sick mind and something not to be taken seriously. However, Clodagh knew him well enough to realise that he had resorted to bluff and humour in order to protect himself from suspecting that there might have been a modicum of truth in those words.

They left their hotel at eight in recently purchased padded

jackets and carrying canvas rucksacks which they had filled with bottled water, binoculars and chocolate, and when they reached the Gazebo on Turret Hill inside the magnificent Dromoland estate and the meeting point for the search, they were both startled and encouraged by the enormous turn out. Men, women and children wrapped up against the early frost together with an assortment of dogs, stout walking sticks, flashlights and walkie-talkies scattered across the area chatting and greeting neighbours and others they had never met before.

A tall, bald man in a navy duffle-coat waved a bright green flag on a stick high in the air and called for attention.

"Good morning, ladies and gentlemen and thank you all for volunteering to help in the search today. My name is Dec and as you are all aware, Superintendent Doyle from the Garda has given his permission for us to look at other areas beyond the Lough where the coach driver was found. We are also grateful to the management of Dromoland Castle for their permission to meet and disband from this point. What I would like to do is divide the groups into four and to the appointed leader of each group I will supply a map of the immediate area."

With the assistance of a young, gangly boy with a wild crop of ginger hair and a plump woman in a pink bobble hat Dec divided the party into roughly sixty people per group suggesting that they each choose a leader. While the discussions were taking place, he surprised Clodagh and Silas by announcing. "We are delighted to have with us today Mr. Silas Murphy and Miss Clodagh Trevor whom I'm sure you all know are the two lead dancers in Arcanum and who have offered to help search for their friends and colleagues."

A gasp of surprise followed by a burst of applause invited them to acknowledge the crowd with a wave of embarrassment as Dec beamed and continued his instructions.

"Group One…" He pointed at the first cluster of people. "Will go to Garrauncam Bridge." He nodded to the bobble-hat who struggled through the mass to pass their leader a map. "Group Two will be in Feakle and if you are going down as far as where the pasture turns to rushes, please do be careful. Group Three will take the area around Bunratty Castle and I shall lead Group four to Quin."

A helicopter flew low overhead and drowned out the last of his words. He shaded his eyes and looked up, then turned back to the crowd.

"Something we have to contend with, I'm afraid. The Gardai and tv news teams will be up there following us."

A hand shot up. "What if we find anything? Do we contact you?"

Dec nodded. "Some of you have walkie-talkies and most of you have mobiles. My numbers are on the map. Call me if there is something significant otherwise don't bother. I'm sure that the locals among you know that in certain parts we might not be able to get a signal or make contact."

"Shall we meet back here?"

"I will be returning to the hotel but it's not obligatory if you find it easier to make it back to your homes from your search area. The management has generously offered to supply tea and coffee if you do return here, but I would be reminding you that at this time of the year it starts getting dark around three-thirty so please be away from the remotest areas by then."

Clodagh and Silas were in Dec's group and en route to the village of Quin. They knew little about it and were filled in as they began their walk through open meadows and pastureland steeped in history and encompassing around forty townlands of old Gaelic origin pre-dating the Norman invasion. It seemed that Quin abbey was considered to be one of the finest and most complete remnants of monastic antiquity and the area was also an archaeologist's paradise having delivered up an important quantity of prehistoric gold.

Members of the group began to fan out and although their chatter was upbeat it was clear they would not lose sight of their serious objective. Parting bushes, prodding with their sticks, they tried to ignore the drone of the helicopters moving backwards and forwards overhead as they pursued their quest with vigour and determination.

It was then that Clodagh began to experience a curious sense of weightlessness, gratifyingly welcome after the melancholia which had become so much part of her daily existence but nonetheless bewildering. The frosty grass felt springy beneath her trainers and the further they walked the less weary and more energised she became.

It was though everything she was seeing and touching was dissolving into her very being, resulting in a heightened awareness of the elements but a sense of detachment from what was happening around her. Voices swam in her ears, Silas and Dec in intense conversation, the occasional laugh or shout or bark almost magnified and somewhere else totally. Vaguely comparable to the experience of coming round from anaesthetic after having her appendix removed as a child. An odd sensation but not a frightening one. There and yet not there. Certainly alone, maybe without identity.

She couldn't remember when she last laughed but had a desire to do so now and wondered if this was what it was like to have taken some sort of hallucinogenic drug. The indigo curtain sweeping across the mountains, the cold clouds bubbling up and chasing the day and the piping birdsong were all part of the one-ness which she was now experiencing and strangely enjoying.

She inhaled the cool air deeply and felt even stronger. Now, as the group neared the area around the abbey, she realised they had all been walking for almost two hours and that she had lost all sense of time.

"Take a break." She heard Dec call out and the search party slowed to a halt then sank thankfully onto the low and ancient stone monoliths in the shadow of the gothic ruins to drink from their flasks and eat their sandwiches.

She was aware that she might be emitting some kind of vibe that whispered to be left alone, for even Silas was keeping his distance. She had no desire to be unfriendly but as she sipped from her water bottle and nibbled on a piece of dark chocolate she knew without knowing why, that she would have to break away and wander her own path in pursuit of the truth behind the mystery that had left such a unique mark on their lives.

★

Peter Sheridan, the consultant psychiatrist, was an albino. Everything about him was milky white and in his hospital coat he almost seemed to disappear into himself. His eyes were pink with deep red pupils and Joe Tierney hated himself for thinking that if he were Dennis Ahearne he'd be even more terrified than he already was discovering Sheridan at his bedside.

The press had caught on and had followed Ahearne's wife and his son Luke to the hospital unit that morning. A newspaper had offered her money for a story, but as she explained to Joe Tierney and Gerry Doyle, she had so little to say that it simply wasn't worth it.

Sheridan flicked down his plastic venetians obliterating the crowd outside and offered chairs to the two detectives and the Ahearnes. He came to the point swiftly, while presenting X-ray results for them to pass around.

"The results from the PET scan show no apparent physical malfunction of the brain. The psychotic disorder from which he appears to be suffering is strongly suggestive of schizophrenia and that accounts for the delusions, mainly persecutory, which he firmly believes to be real."

Mrs. Ahearne stared at the film image in bewilderment and passed it to her son.

"But he has never suffered from schizophrenia. Why should he now?"

Sheridan shook his pale head and sank into his high-backed swivel chair. "That is what we are trying to establish, Mrs. Ahearne. We have seen cases like this before but they are rare. They can be triggered by external pressures which are not the result of an injury but which affect the orbitofrontal area of the brain, an area which is still demanding further research and exploration."

"So, whoever he encountered and is responsible for the kidnapping shocked him into something similar to schizophrenia?" Joe Tierney enquired.

"That would be the trigger in this case. Almost certainly, yes."

"So what is the prognosis and how do you treat it?" asked Gerry Doyle.

"As far as the treatment is concerned we tailor for the individual so it will be a combination of therapy and medication. Dennis needs support and care to help him recover from the shock he has experienced. I have no doubt that in time he will regain his faculties, his moments of clarity lead me to believe this. Meanwhile, we have to wait until that time comes."

He rose from behind his desk, a cue that their meeting was over.

"How we going to handle the press?" Luke Ahearne asked Joe Tierney. "They won't give up following us around."

"I'll release a statement saying that your dad is unable to give us any information at the present time due to his medical condition. I would also appreciate if you do not mention the meeting with the dancers yesterday. We have to tread very carefully so as not to allow the mounting hysteria and conspiracy theories to flourish."

The young man nodded. "I understand."

They each shook hands with Peter Sheridan who agreed to keep them in touch with any new developments and bracing themselves for the onslaught of cameras and questions they hurried to their respective cars.

★

Blue faded to grey as the day melted and Clodagh continued her now solitary journey of hope. Fields and pastureland stretched endlessly into the far horizon each forming part of a repeating pattern trodden without weariness or limit of endurance.

The sweet woody aroma of burning leaves filled her senses and for the first time since leaving Dromoland she checked her watch. Nearly three. Soon she would have to return but she told herself that a little further would make no difference.

She paused beside a tiny rivulet and caught her reflection in its silver water mirror. Was it her imagination or did a streak of pale blue light briefly appear across her image? Dismissing it, she carried on, becoming aware of distant voices and peals of merry laughter accompanied by the unmistakeable sound of a fiddle.

She blinked as she saw them coming down the hilly slope towards her. A group of young men and women in brightly coloured clothes of another era, carrying long silk ribbons which fluttered in the wind. One of the women beat a tambourine and the man beside her held a stone bottle and a goblet while he danced to the music.

Every one of them wore make-up and the women's scent was heady and intoxicating. They allowed their long hair to blow free, thrusting out tightly corseted chests and laughing from their ruby painted lips as they grew closer.

Clodagh held her breath as one of the women brushed against her, greeting her in Irish. "Dia dhuit."

The man who had been holding the goblet and bottle now poured a trickle of liquid and offered it to Clodagh. "Honey mead." He told her. "Sup."

Almost trancelike, Clodagh raised the goblet to her lips and allowed the sweet wine to act as an elixir to her mellowed spirit.

"Who are you?" She whispered.

The man removed his tricorn hat with a bow. "We're the entertainers for the medieval banquet up at the Castle this evening. Do come."

"I can't. I'm sorry." Clodagh stammered. "I have to get back to Ennis."

"Shame." He studied her face curiously as he took the goblet from her hands. "Beidh lá maith."

She watched them wend their way across the fields towards the castle, their voices blending in a haunting madrigal which lingered in the late afternoon air for a magic moment then disappeared with them behind a trail of silk ribbons.

Now darkness was threatening and she quickened her steps back along the path she had remembered coming. Much of it was downhill which made it easier and she was pleased to note that her strange burst of energy had not yet deserted her.

After an hour she reached Rosroe, passing the prehistoric tombs that surrounded the lake gleaming and still in the silent evening light, and paused to offer up a spoken, fragmented prayer for Sinead and the rest of her friends, as simple as the prayers of her childhood, pleading once again for their safe return.

She didn't jump when the beam from a torch interrupted her and Silas appeared quietly at her side, his familiar presence indicating comfort and safety.

"Where did you get to? I was worried to death."

He really was worried. She could see it in his eyes. "I'm sorry," she told him. "I had to break away."

"That's alright." He told her gently. "But you've got to be careful. I don't want to have to report you missing as well."

"Did they find anything?" She asked, knowing full well what his answer would be.

He shook his head. "Nope. As they say, tomorrow is another day."

They linked arms as Silas shone his torch along the murky footpath leading to the town where they would catch their bus back to Ennis, when Clodagh suddenly stopped, noticing what appeared to be a small flat item on the ground close to their feet. Releasing her arm from his she bent down to pluck it from its resting place and held it against the light to examine exactly what she had found.

"What is it?" Silas asked her. "Some kind of card?"

"Yes." Clodagh answered quietly. "But not just any card. Look…"

Silas peered closer and then stared at Clodagh in disbelief. "A Tarot card? Can it really be a Tarot card?"

The enigmatic robed figure of the High Priestess stared back at them under the torchlight, faded and yet discernable.

Clodagh's paralysis was instant, as gooseflesh seemed to begin in the column of her rigid spine, flooding outward, covering her shoulders and arms and racing down her thighs. This is no coincidence, she thought wildly. This is something else. Something beyond our understanding.

Silas was still inspecting the card, taking it from her and turning it over in his palm, unaware of her torpidity. "Interesting. Not the Pamela Coleman-Smith design which we copied for our costumes and set."

She knew that he had taken some basic instruction on the tarot from an American psychic while working on the choreography and she tried to make sense of his words as he pressed on, clearly excited by the discovery.

"No, this is a card design of the oldest surviving tarot deck from the Italian Renaissance. Probably painted around 1400. Clodagh, this is one of the Triumphs, the Trionfi."

As he spoke the dusk deepened and unease floated in as suddenly as the dark wings of a preying bird. He caught Clodagh's fearful expression and immediately wrapped her in his arms.

She knew he wanted to kiss her like a lover now and she allowed it to happen. The chill disappeared in an instant and the heat of desire took its place. He began to kiss away the tears that had crept down her cheeks and she returned his kisses hungrily, drawing him in, touching and kindling his eager body until he was on fire, hard and urgent against her. Their rucksacks hit the ground as she stumbled backwards, he not letting her fall, guiding her towards the trunk of an oak where they tore off their clothes, exploring hitherto secret places which they gifted to one another gladly, releasing months of tension and pain. The old tree took the force of their rhythm while diamonds of light pierced the sky and the smell of the rich earth they had disturbed provided the perfect archaism to their coupling.

When it was over they clung to one another, quietly dressed and resumed their journey, for the interval had ended and a new act was beginning.

She was silent, lost in thought, but she knew he was right when he told her.

"So the search starts again. In a very different direction."

★

The mixed emotions that Silas experienced on opening night were many and inextricably linked. The raw agony of missing his dancers seared through him with a new intensity augmented by the fact that the troupe from Lighthouse were clearly overjoyed to be performing and their exhilaration was contagious. His feelings for Clodagh were now in a zone which he wished he could penetrate and define and although he knew they were deep-rooted, he sensed that her desire was not as strong and that he would have to tread carefully on the journey forward. Then there was the fear that their relationship might never resume the familiar ease it had so enjoyed and that particular thought was too depressing for him to even begin to contemplate.

His mind was also still absorbing the extraordinary discovery of the Tarot card and Dennis Ahearne's malevolent outburst. He had already decided that as soon as the show had settled into a comfortable routine he would begin his own investigation with or without the aid of the Gardai but hopefully with the assistance of Clodagh. It was set to be a journey into the unknown which he would map out as best he could with the very few tangible facts at his disposal.

Right now though there was a performance to deliver, and the weight of expectation was bearing heavily on his and Clodagh's shoulders. The press and many local dignitaries would be in the audience tonight and as far as future bookings were concerned Deirdre had told him that every seat had been sold stretching up to and beyond Christmas.

He could hear the crowd clapping along to the beat of the Lighthouse dancers. Safe and traditional stuff that he had left behind but which the audience were embracing fervently and he guessed that they were also in some way extending that embrace towards Arcanum.

He stood in the wings stretching his muscles to the point of pain and watching the line of girls with their shiny, ringletted wigs topped with tiaras and their short bright velvet dresses performing perfectly choreographed slip jigs. Then the boys joined them, almost absurdly uniformed in their white shirts, black ties, vests and black trousers. Erin Shaw was certainly no slouch in picking a tight team, although Silas was aware that her lead dancers were not of the high standard that some of the routines demanded.

He knew that Clodagh's mother and father were in the front row, together with her Auntie Peggy and he had extended the offer of tickets to all the other parents but they had declined. It wasn't hard to understood why for it was obvious that they would have found the whole experience far too harrowing.

When it was time for he and Clodagh to make their entrances in the second half, a hush descended on the auditorium, despite the bar doing great business during the interval. This is what they had all come to see. The young man and woman who, in the physical sense, had not been lost like the others, but who were just as adrift and isolated in their grief and confusion.

Silas took the first set and performed a light fast reel. In his scarlet silk shirt, deep red and black waistcoat and leather trousers he rose, clicked and landed with all the skill and precision he could muster to loud cheers from the crowd. As he danced, his mind returned to that last night in Dublin when he and Clodagh and the troupe had brought the house down with their unique Tarot-based finale.

When Clodagh entered, the cheers subsided. The lights

had dimmed and a blue gel followed her entrance as the haunting reed pipes opened the lilting, specially composed music which Silas had commissioned. An edited version had now been cut to fit the new choreography and he prayed that it would work.

For some reason which was unknown to him, she had ordered a different costume to the one worn originally and the copy of which she had rehearsed in. This new dress was white with a satin top and knee length lace skirt which floated as she moved, disturbing tiny particles of stage dust that twinkled like fireflies around her. A blue sash was tied to her waist in a loose bow and her titian hair was braided as before.

Yet again he was mesmerised by the way she used her body to express herself, creating stage magic of a very special kind, mysterious and ethereal, allowing the audience a glimpse of mind, body and spirit fusing in the art of the dance.

This was something that the audience had rarely witnessed. A purely balletic performance given by an Irish dancer who had moulded the choreography to reflect her inner feelings and emotions.

Time seemed frozen to all who experienced it. She could have been dancing for fifteen minutes or fifteen hours for the effect was spellbinding. But when she bent like a willow into the blue light and the music faded with the lone call of a curlew, there was a pregnant pause before the audience rose to their feet, clapping and cheering the slim figure on the stage who disappeared before their eyes as the lights went to black out.

When they came up again the stage was empty and Silas entered to the steady beat of an Irish drum. As the Diviner he played to a selection of giant cards that formed part of the scenery, the characters on which were originally depicted by his dancers. First The Fool, and his mime and footwork reflected the frenzy and extravagance that the meaning of this card represented. The drum was now joined by the strings of a dozen fiddles as Silas moved from card to card, The Emperor – power and protection, The Hermit – prudence and circumspection and on and on until he has translated the unspoken symbolism offered to an unseen Enquirer and members of the audience through dance.

Punctuated by wild bursts of applause, Silas was drawing the routine to a close. He paused before the empty throne of the High Priestess, the only figure he had not acknowledged, as Clodagh glided slowly in behind him wearing a hooded blue robe.

He turned to face her before embarking on a flexuous step dance then slowed to a different pace as she whirled around him, an enigmatic moth circling a flame. While he, the Diviner, struggled to convey her mystery and wisdom, she positioned herself quietly upon the throne as the sound of a final solitary drum echoed like a heart-beat and Silas's head bowed in prayer.

Once again there was a lull before the storm of approval and as the two dancers moved to the front of the stage to take their bows they could almost touch the emotion written on the faces of the crowd standing and cheering in front of them. Clodagh's mother and her Auntie Peggy were crying freely as they hugged one another and when two young dancers from Lighthouse entered from either side of the stage with giant sprays of peach roses, purple thistles and lilies, a roar ascended to the rafters which Silas could have sworn was loud enough to reach Dublin's fair city.

They'd pulled it off. Somehow they had taken the dangerous risk of performing as a duo rather than as a twenty-six strong team, simplifying, altering and infusing their technique and skills to produce a rich, awe-inspiring shared experience which was nothing short of miraculous.

But now, challenges of another kind awaited them.

★

76

CO. CLARE.
1735

The black dog raised its head as the crackling fire hissed out a shower of sparks that landed close to its front paws.

The young woman wrapped in a rug and curled in the chair opposite stared at the dog and growled, inciting the animal to growl back with undisguised venom.

Kathleen Dooley stretched and yawned, pushing her hair out of her eyes and with a sinking heart realised that another day of imprisonment was drawing to a close and a life once filled with freedom and laughter was fading as swiftly as the autumn light.

It had been three weeks now since Mick Gilligan and his wife Sarah had taken her in after the horrible tragedy brought upon her by her husband Thomas's selfish and unexpected death. Three weeks in which they and their spotty faced son Brendan had bestowed their self-righteous hospitality upon the poor widow woman who had been left with nothing but a few clothes, a powder box and some toothpicks to her name.

And what a name Dooley had now become for local gossip and derision since the news of his suicide reached the God-fearing people of the village. Everything seemed to have happened so quickly. She had arrived home after a day filled with sexual pleasures to find a crowd gathered outside the house who hissed and spat at her as she rushed inside, only to find the cold dead body of her husband lying on the kitchen table and guarded by the farmer Mick Gilligan.

The next few days passed in a blur as strangers marched in and out hardly acknowledging her presence. First, the Sheriff of Clare's men to take away the body for which she begged to be allowed a Christian burial but which was threateningly refused. Then the chief Smith of the county who advised her that the cottage and forge would now pass into the hands of another blacksmith to be appointed as soon as was possible. That didn't seem fair to Kathleen. Not fair at all. Thomas had built up his thriving and successful business through the sweat of his own labour and now it was almost as though he had never existed, for his boots seemed so rapidly easy to fill.

Then the final indignity which lead to her downfall and came about through a mixture of ill fortune and bad judgement.

Blinded by passion and his powers of persuasion, she had allowed her golden haired lover to share the marital bed. One morning, wakened from their early slumber by a loud banging on the door, they were confronted by a dwarf-like official in a crooked grey wig who had entered the house and mounted the stairs to the bedroom. Unable to tear his weasel eyes away from her bare breasts he had bawled at her for an hour, whereupon she had screamed back at him and the damage had been final and irreversible.

Through tears of despair she later learned that because of the criminal offence her husband had committed by killing himself and what the judge had described as her ill-behaviour and inability to fulfil her obligations as a decent law-abiding widow, she would be forced to forfeit all inherited property and finance to the King and the Church.

Thus Kathleen Dooley now found herself homeless and poverty stricken. Her lover had fled and because her parents were no longer alive, the Gilligans were her only salvation in a harsh and sadistic environment that blamed her for her husband's death and also for the loss of their dance master. But she kept telling herself that her loss was greater, for she had no home and missed the latter with a longing that ached inside her night and day.

Also, she reflected bitterly, she had loved dancing too, and certainly her life would be more bearable now if she could dance away her woes to the music of a blind fiddler in Gilligan's barn. But it seemed more than likely that he would never resume his obligation and where there had once been boundless energy there was now apathy. The dancing had ceased and with it the pleasures they had all enjoyed as part of their daily existence.

The sound of pots and pans rattling in the kitchen signalled that Sarah Gilligan was preparing supper for Mick and his son when they returned from the fields and the thought of having to listen to an account of another of their boring working days was just too dull to contemplate.

Realising she would have to go in and somehow endure the tedium the evening promised, she opened the door that led to the kitchen then almost fainted with surprise.

There at the table, seated like an invited guest and grinning toothlessly at the amazement on her face, was the old woman who had served the previous Master. And laid out in front of her were not the anticipated plates, forks and knives but a selection of cards from the Tarot. The cards of the Major Arcana.

★

Blossom Fayard signed off from the Skype call she had received from her old neighbourhood pal Silas Murphy and immediately went online to book a plane ticket to take her across the Atlantic to Shannon airport the following day.

It had been a long time since they had spoken. Three years. And although they had just been enjoying a conversation on camera, it was very different from meeting in person.

Throughout his call, Silas had repeatedly referred to her as Billy, then apologised for his carelessness, but Blossom understood that her friend was under considerable stress and she found no problem in his taking time to come to terms with the change. After all, many of her friends, neighbours and customers in Boston, not to mention her own family, still had trouble acclimatising to such a radical transformation.

The surgery had been successful. At first. Then complications set in which necessitated another two operations followed by chronic pain control management administered intravenously, months of bed rest and numerous physical and psychological evaluations.

During that time she had turned to her inner muse and took spiritual comfort from her power to bypass the usual sensory channels and transcend mundane reality. She gave thanks for those gifts and for the fact that her heightened five senses which had shaped her daily life for as long as she could remember had not been limited by the invasive procedures her material form had endured.

She also gave credit to her parents for their patience and devotion during that difficult period, knowing that whatever powers she possessed were in part inherited from their individual genetic make-up. Her mother being of Irish descent, had entertained her as a child with colourful stories of goblins and ghosts in mystical far away places and her father, a Haitian, had often terrified and enhanced her visual imagery with his tales of black magic and voodoo practiced in the village in which he had grown up.

She had missed Arcanum's opening in Dublin and it had been heart breaking. Having known Silas for so long and educating him on the history and symbolism of the Tarot for what she considered to be an exciting creative concept, she could only communicate with him by Skype and e-mail, devouring the wonderful photographs of the show and following the press enthusiasm from her hospital bed.

When news broke of the disappearance of the dancers she was as shocked and puzzled as the rest of the world and when her body became stronger she tried to reach him by phone but found it impossible. Short texts and e-mails flittered between them but as the weeks went by and there was no sign of progress, Blossom had almost given up hope that she could help in any way. She had visited his parents to try and add some comfort to their concern, for they too had been unable to enjoy lengthy conversations with their son while such uncertainty in his life persisted.

Now her friend had rung. He and his lead girl dancer needed her, he said. Some odd things had happened and she was the only person they could turn to.

So of course, she had to go.

★

CO. CLARE.
1735

"Mallacht!!" Mick Gilligan shouted again at the old woman. "Mallacht!" ("A Curse!")

"Dia linn go léir!" ("God help us all!")

Standing in the middle of the large turf-fired kitchen he watched the colour of his wife's face drain to ash, Kathleen Dooley's hand fly to her mouth and heard his son utter a nervous high-pitched laugh.

He shook his head, uncertain as to what to do next. He had brought the hag here to try and extract anything from her that would explain the desolation that had befallen the community since the new Dance Master had departed without a word of explanation or before fulfilling his duty to appoint another Master in his place.

He had never heard her speak, so after feeding her slices of his best ham and cheese and loosening her tongue with a cup of mead, he was then confounded by a torrent of primitive Irish which he had great difficulty deciphering as she spoke of the night that the old Dance Master had died.

This verbal display had been suspended periodically by her fascination with the pack of cards which she constantly shuffled and selected, then laid out in front of them. The most prominent of which now rested on the top of the pack and to which she pointed, nodding her head, expecting all in the room to understand its significance.

The colourful card pictured a young man in almost identical clothes to those worn by the Dance Master, even down to the upturned shoes. He was fair in complexion and seated at a desk covered with ritual objects. This, Mick Gilligan endeavoured to translate as best he could from her broken words and gesticulations, was The Magician, a manipulator who created change, a trickster and more mysteriously one who brought the dead to life.

He tried to keep his patience but it wasn't easy. For most

of the time the woman's eyes, if they weren't on the cards, were closed as if she were in a trance and when she uttered her final dramatic pronouncement, they widened terrifyingly to add more chill to the strange proceedings.

She described her Master's deathbed message in a gibberish which he only realised when she had finished was probably Latin and the one word he could pick up on was 'maledictio' which was easily translated into Irish as a curse. In other words, their old Dance Master had uttered an appeal or prayer for ill fortune to fall upon one or more persons for eternity if his legacy was not continued.

The old woman, clearly exhausted by her efforts and replete from the first good meal she had eaten in a long while, then laid her head on the table and slept.

Mick Gilligan tried to consider what his next move would be. He wouldn't know where to begin looking for a new Master. As far as his limited knowledge was concerned they were always chosen by the local predecessor, were fiercely territorial and were expected to possess a certain standard of expertise and discipline. It had reached his ears that certain jig actors roamed the countryside masquerading as Dance Masters but they were temperamental and unreliable fellows with very few skills and only able to perform the most basic of steps.

No, however hard it might to be to achieve, somehow he had to persuade this boy to return to face his responsibilities and was still baffled and angered by his careless attitude. After all, could he not see that it was in his interest? He had a curse on his head, the consequences of which he had seemingly ignored, and in so doing was dragging good and honest folk down with him.

But how to persuade him? Certainly not with more money for there was none in the pot. And it was impossible to compete with the Earls and Lords for whom Gilligan had heard he was now working.

He glanced across the kitchen, past his wife Sarah washing the plates and pans, past his son who was dipping bread into his soup and devouring it noisily and past the woman, now snoring like one of his old sows and with her head still resting on the table.

Kathleen Dooley was winding her hair around her fingers, lost in what seemed like the dark night of the soul. She had pushed her dish of food away untouched and Gilligan felt a sudden pang of sympathy for the young woman whose infatuation had changed her from a playful, well-fed kitten into a scarred and suspicious wild animal with nowhere to hide.

And yet the existence of that infatuation was the only card he had left to play. He would have to convince her to entice the boy back with her own particular brand of magnetism which Gilligan was sure that he was too weak a character to resist. In addition, she would instil in him a real and dreaded fear of the power of the curse placed on him that night in the dying man's house and which they had all now learned about from the old woman.

But there was one other component in the final framework of the plan, which would either send him running for the hills or literally facing the music, for Kathleen Dooley was with child.

*

With the euphoria of their first night over, Clodagh was looking forward to meeting Billy Fayard, spoken of with affection and respect by Silas and whom she had heard so much about over the years. Of course he was not called Billy now but Blossom and he had become a she.

Clodagh was intrigued, as she had never known anyone who had undergone a gender change and wasn't quite sure what to expect, particularly as Silas had told her about the difficult time his friend had gone through to achieve the transition. But when they both arrived in the hotel bar straight from the airport and she rose to greet them, it wasn't the pancake make-up and false eyelashes that she first noticed, but the aura of rainbow energy that generated around Blossom's beautiful dark head and which it was clear that no-one but herself could see.

Silas made the introductions and she and Blossom exchanged light kisses then settled into the armchairs as he ordered coffee and almond croissants. She had little time to recover from what she had witnessed but wondered if Blossom was looking at her in a way that indicated that she too might have picked up on some similar emanation.

Not wishing to dwell on this unexpected aspect of their meeting, Clodagh knew that they had to get down to the business for which Blossom had made the journey across the Atlantic. She allowed Silas to do most of the talking as he recaptured the stormy night when he had seen the dancers off in the bus, then lowered his voice as he betrayed Joe Tierney's request for not divulging what they had heard from the driver.

The coffee arrived and was duly poured as their visitor removed her vivid orange raincoat, revealing a low scooped-neck black dress accessorised by a number of delicate silver chains. Clodagh noticed with interest that her cleavage was almost flawless apart from a few dark moles dotted across honey-brown skin and her long legs, encased in black fishnet, were possibly the most shapely she had ever seen on any woman.

Blossom interrupted only when she needed Silas to emphasize a point and Clodagh was surprised and impressed that someone who was so obviously a psychic healer and teller of fortunes was anxious to examine the possibility of rational explanations before offering up her own suggestions based on her particular skills.

"This Tarot card you found interests me deeply," she said, addressing them both. Can I see it please?"

Clodagh had put it into a clean envelope for safe-keeping and now placed it on the table between them.

Blossom took the envelope and slid out the card, studying it intently then laying it in the palm of one hand while stroking it with the other. She closed her eyes for what seemed to them like minutes but was probably closer to thirty seconds.

"You're right, Silas. This is certainly one of the Visconti-Sforza deck, but what is fascinating me is that the card itself is very old."

"Really? How old?" Silas asked, puzzled.

"Hard to say, but I would hazard a guess at 18th century, maybe earlier."

Clodagh was stunned. "But how can that be? It's in such good condition."

"Yes, it is." Blossom answered. "But let's disregard its age for the moment. Why do you think you were the ones who found it?"

Silas jumped in first. "I think it's a message from the kidnappers. They know about Arcanum, they know it's the name of the troupe and of our set dance. It's a tease of some description, but I can't begin to understand why they would do something like that."

Blossom nodded then turned her attention solely to Clodagh. "And you, Clodagh. What is your take on this?"

Clodagh felt her cheeks begin to burn before she answered. Then without any warning from either her heart or her brain, she found herself blurting out everything about her dream, the mysterious healing of her injury and the strange discomfort with the costume. When she had finished, she sat back in her seat while her face slowly retained its normal colour. "I don't know whether it's got anything to do with this. Sorry."

There was silence for a moment as Silas tried to absorb what she had just told them and Blossom digested it with a nod of the head, her eyes now firmly fixed on the girl.

"So the High Priestess is the link here. The Tarot and specifically The High Priestess. Secrets, mystery, the future as yet unrevealed. Someone is sending you a message, Clodagh."

Clodagh experienced the same cold shivers she had felt the night they had found the card and repeated almost word for word what she had uttered in her dream. "But why me? What message?"

Blossom placed her coffee cup carefully back on its saucer and leaned forward with an urgency of tone. "I'm trying to connect the dots, Clodagh. It's not just you. But you are an integral part of an overall grand design or plan. Don't forget that the driver said 'they wanted Silas.' Someone is trying to get a message to both of you but you each have very individual psychic make-ups. Your seven energy centres are totally different. Yours, Silas, like many humans, are closed or un-awakened, allowing only the barest amount of vibrational current necessary for functioning. Clodagh…" she paused and took the girl's hand. "The knots binding your soul are freeing themselves quite rapidly. Your seven chakras are opening and making you feel as though you radiate from within and are capable of achieving anything that you desire. Am I right?"

Clodagh nodded with an overwhelming sense of relief. At last someone - this new and extraordinary person had put precisely what she had been experiencing into words. She had read about these seven energy centres but never really understood their meaning in relation to her own physical or spiritual self. Somehow, maybe through dance, she had released this centred energy by which the soul was thought to be connected to the body. It could explain the dream occurring on the night of the disappearance, the long walk which she had done without fatigue, and the Tarot dance in its modified form wearing clothes which did not inhibit her, for while portraying the intuitive and mysterious figure of the Major Arcana she was also retaining her individuality as the figure in her dream had advised.

She looked across at Silas who was staring at her in bewilderment and felt sorry that Blossom had somehow unwittingly divided and separated them in this way.

"What do we do now?" she heard herself asking.

"I certainly don't believe this is a straightforward abduction by human forces." Blossom answered. "Therefore I'd like to visit Rosroe and the surrounding area as soon as possible. Could we do that today?"

"I'll get the car." Silas said, reaching for his jacket. "If we set off now we can be back in time for the show."

"I'll go check in and freshen up." Blossom told them. "And get out of these killer heels."

Despite the November chill there were many people milling around when they arrived at the bridge that led to the lake area. There was also a television camera crew setting up and Silas explained that the charity Facebook page for missing persons was attracting much attention from volunteers who were willing to give up their time to participate in area searches stretching from the town of Newmarket-on-Fergus and beyond.

Yellow ribbons, that now familiar symbol of hope of a safe return, were tied to trees and lamp-posts and streamed through the air like a flock of golden winged birds almost as far as the eye could see. The innocuous sight of an out of season ice-cream van parked behind a Garda patrol car reminded them of the continuous volume of curious visitors regularly flooding through the town, as well as the on-going police presence, sadly no nearer to their goal than they had been three months earlier.

Blossom, now cosily ensconced in a black puffer jacket, jeans and thick walking boots had done her research. As they walked, she took on the mantle of a tour guide, remarking in an amazingly knowledgeable way about the Neolithic and ancient Celtic history of the area, the complexity of the ley-lines which ran between the Burren and a town called Clonmacnoise situated on the Shannon and revealed her study of the old local rural townlands, many of them pre-dating the Norman invasion.

When they reached the footpath near the lake where they had discovered the card, most of the other walkers continued their way further up the hill towards the castle ruins so that they were now a lone trio in a landscape already touched by the long fingers of an early afternoon mist rising from the still water.

To her concern, Clodagh suddenly noticed that Blossom was crying. Large tears ran down her face streaking mascara as they slid towards her chin before dropping like dark raindrops on to the collar of her coat.

"Blossom, what is it? What's the matter?" Clodagh moved to comfort her while Silas looked hesitant, unsure as to how to react to a friend whom he knew so well and yet now appeared so different.

Blossom produced a man's large cotton handkerchief from her coat pocket and wiped her face, then looked around as though aware of some invisible force.

"There is so much sadness here." She told them in a low voice which they strained to hear. "It's tangible and it's reaching out to me. To us."

"The place is full of history going way back in time." Silas said gently. "I'm not surprised that someone like you can feel it."

Blossom shook her head. "It's not just that. Somebody or something is trying to make contact. Of that I'm sure."

"Should we go?" asked Clodagh. "Is it frightening you? If so, we should leave."

"No, no. It's not frightening or hostile. It's pleading, appealing to us for help. Desperate I would say."

"Is it the dancers?" Silas asked her, looking suddenly anxious. "If so, can we communicate with them in some way?"

As Clodagh waited expectantly for Blossom to answer, she realised with a degree of unease that the mist from the lake was starting to creep ever closer to the spot where they were standing. Not just the bog-standard Irish greyness any longer but a pale silvery presence which threatened to entirely surround them blotting out the rest of the landscape.

The dislocation that she felt now was different from what she had experienced on her last visit. Mainly because everything was so unnaturally quiet. Not a bird could be heard nor even a rustling from the trees. It was as though she was passing through a threshold of utter silence.

Then the mist cleared, leaving everything stripped of its colour, a light honey hue which reminded her of old photographs she had seen as a child in the local library. She was aware that all three of them were standing in the same spot, but as she looked down towards the road and the town beyond she could tell at once that something was wrong. Releasing a gasp of astonishment, she realised that there was no road and no town.

The hedge that divided the fields from the road was there but what had been the road was now a wide, unmade up dirt track. There was no bridge and not one of the three church spires that were there previously could be seen rising against the skyline. She could make out only a handful of thatched cottages dotted sparsely in the area where the town had been and set amongst acres of pastureland on which cattle and sheep now grazed.

Her heart almost stopped as she saw a figure driving a horse and cart slowly along the bumpy track. Although he was quite a distance away, she could see that he was old and had thick whiskered sideburns and a shock of greasy hair. He was wearing a leather waistcoat and filthy boots and she could have sworn that he glanced up in her direction, then shook his head as if in disbelief and rode on.

It was impossible to measure the experience as far as the passage of time was concerned and almost as soon as Clodagh had recorded the snapshot in her mind, the silver mist rolled in again then evaporated, leaving her trembling.

Silas was the first to speak, his voice hoarse with amazement. "What was that? Can someone tell me what the hell just happened there?"

Clodagh ran towards him and took his hand. "You saw it too. Oh, thank God."

They both looked towards the woman beside them to provide the answers and who seemed to be glowing, her eyes bright with a strange excitement.

"Well, you guys. Whoever would have believed it? And of course nobody will. We've all just experienced our first time slip!"

★

He knew at once that she hadn't written the note, for Kathleen Dooley was illiterate. The coarse piece of paper sat on his table and he re-read it with a mixture of curiosity and frustration. The writing seemed to comprise of two completely different styles. One, scrawled and withered then changing to bold black-inked capital letters which were more than a little threatening.

It had to be the farmer Gilligan who had sent this missive on her behalf. Its contents were a stark five lines.

A matter of life and death.
Remember the Curse.
Come Soon.
You will be rewarded well.
Love. K

There were many reasons why he should ignore it, mainly because he didn't need these people any longer. They had served their purpose in terms of free food and drink and what dull learners most of them were in the matter of the dance.

His appetite was now well provided for following his lessons at the big houses but he had not yet managed to seduce the flame haired harper whom he was now encountering there on a regular basis. She was, it seemed, only bestowing her favours on the gentry and although at times her eyes held unspoken promises during those civilised musical evenings, he was no closer to introducing her to his own instrument which was well practiced and ready to give service.

Despite his unrequited lust, it was Kathleen who without question knew how to play him and he recalled with pleasure her wild laughter, her unpredictability and her stamina to stay the course during days and nights of constant fornication. But she had become a liability. He had been publicly humiliated when officials descended on her house and had kept a safe distance since the day he had been discovered in her bed.

It was now obvious that she wanted to continue their tryst and had thus instructed Gilligan to pen the cryptic letter. But he was baffled by the mention of some stupid curse. Surely she couldn't be referring to the ramblings of the senile old Master on his deathbed. He had taken little notice of it at the time, having been so enamoured with the most lavish costume he had ever seen, that he couldn't remember the content of the words uttered.

His attention was diverted by the sight of a large spider spinning its silvery web between the rough stone wall and the head of his bed. Mesmerised by the ingenuity of it he wondered if this was what he was being drawn into? Some sort of trap designed to keep him dancing to their tune. He looked around the hovel that had been his home for the past few months, knowing it was time to move on. He had suffered enough verbal abuse from the locals and from the rotten fruit and vegetables being hurled daily at his door. Perhaps he should return to County Galway where the old man had found him and offer his services to the large houses there. At least he would be able to provide references of value now and with the money he had earned could afford to pick and choose rather than wasting his time tutoring the under-privileged. If he moved stealthily and without notice, he would avoid having to pass on his talents to a new Master.

But what to do about Kathleen? Maybe he would go to the barn one last time, take her down on a bed of hay and give her the satisfaction she craved. In fact, he felt as horny as a spring cock just thinking about it. For once it was a clear dry night and he made the decision to take the brisk walk to Gilligan's farm and then at daybreak fly the coop.

★

Silas found his mind wandering during the performance that night. Inhabiting another character and with applause once more ringing in his ears it seemed as though everything that had happened earlier was just another scene change in another show, but one that was totally unrehearsed.

He was also mulling over Clodagh's revelations. Now he could understand the added layer of preoccupation that she had been demonstrating since the disappearance and wished that she had shared them with him.

If they hadn't all witnessed it, then this morning's events would have convinced him that he had finally flipped, the stresses and strains of the past few months having taken their toll and only the sterile environment of Dennis Ahearne's medical facility would be his best option.

But Blossom had made the incident appear to be just another one of those things in life to be experienced either by luck or by choice. Like watching a sunset in Kuala Lumpur or sky-diving over a steaming volcano in Iceland. You either get to see it or you don't but it doesn't mean it isn't there.

She explained to him and to Clodagh that time slips had been frequently catalogued by people from different backgrounds and in various countries over the years and that the time-phenomenon was something which had been studied by physicists and writers from Einstein and H. G. Wells to Stephen Hawking. She was not going to play with their minds discussing quantum physics but putting it as simply as she could, at the centre of it all was the existence of energy which might perhaps survive in another dimension where the concept of past, present and future differs from our slavish devotion to the calendar and the clock. She told them that when encountered, albeit unconsciously by a person or persons, that moment in time could play like a recorded image. What they had witnessed was an instance of retro cognition and precognition. Through a tear in the fabric of time they were all peering into the past which was retro cognition. The stranger in the cart who looked up and apparently saw them would have experienced precognition. In other words seeing into the future.

Silas had to ask "Why us? Why has no-one else reported this happening in that particular spot?"

"Because we were giving out a very powerful energy at that moment." Blossom replied. "We were avidly searching for answers there and I am certain that is why we experienced the dislocation. And who's to say no-one else has experienced it? Many wouldn't report it for fear of ridicule."

"So, are you saying it's connected to the disappearance?" Clodagh ventured.

Blossom nodded. "I'm convinced of it. Somehow there's a connection which I'm still trying to work out."

"And you think the Tarot plays a part in all this?" Silas probed, struggling to hold on to logical thought and failing miserably.

"Of course." Blossom suddenly looked tired. "I'm jet-lagged guys. I'll go catch a nap and see you at the show tonight." And that was where they had left it.

As they came off stage, Silas led Clodagh into his dressing room.

"So, what do you think? Is Blossom on the right track?"

Clodagh nodded. "I'm sure she is. However bewildering it is to us right now, if anyone's going to get our dancers back she will."

He so much wanted to tell her he loved her at that moment that the intensity of his feelings alarmed him. His nerves were still on edge and he knew that he was in danger of blowing it. But needing to understand how she felt, he said it, then immediately felt better. Out in the open where it belonged and to hell with the consequences.

She moved forward and touched his cheek with her fingers, looking at him with such tenderness that for one brief moment his spirits soared.

"And I love you too, Silas." She told him gently. "But not in the way you want me to."

He longed to ask why, but realised it would probably

come out sounding like a petulant whine, so he just said. "That's a shame. I think we would have been really good together."

"But we are." She kissed his brow this time, raising hopes which were once again to be dashed. "You're my best friend and we work together brilliantly. I have never been as close to anyone as I am to you and probably never will be."

He studied her for a moment, then turned away to uncork a bottle of wine knowing that Blossom would be joining them soon and needing to have just a few more moments to try and learn what it was that she wanted from life.

"How do you see your future?" He asked, handing her a glass and clinking it against his in a mock toast.

She shook her head, smiling at his directness. "I know what I don't see. I don't see Clodagh married lady with two kids and a car in the garage and a regular husband."

"Do you want to become a nun?" In trying to understand, he knew he was going about it in a clumsy way but it was too late to retract the question now.

This time her smile turned to laughter. "No, Silas, I do not want to be a nun. What I do see, or rather what I hope for, is to continue dancing for as long as I can and maybe contribute any talent I might have to those who need it. Dancing is my life and always will be."

"So you want to teach?"

"Maybe. Silas, I have so many random thoughts racing through my mind with all the strange things that are going on that I can only see my life in the present."

He didn't want her to feel she was in any way under pressure and so drew the conversation to a reluctant close with what he hoped were not cheesy sentiments.

"I just want you to know that whatever path you decide to follow, mine will never be far away."

Her laughter faded and with tears glistening in her eyes she gave him the gentle kiss of a soul-mate, their night of impulsive passion now seeming as distant as the vision of another century glimpsed earlier that day.

"Thank you." She said simply. "That means everything."

★

"What about the swear-box?" Joe Tierney heard his wife yell on her way upstairs as he switched off the television uttering yet another expletive. "I knew you wouldn't last the year."

A new year's resolution made all too rashly many months ago and it took this crazy case to break it. But really this was the last straw to add to the ever growing pile of shite that was being heaped upon him, his colleagues in Clare and his team of conscientious detectives and uniform who were working day and night to try and crack it.

The tabloids worldwide were having a field day and he wondered if he could really blame them for unleashing their lynch mob mentality given the circumstances. While there was no-one being held accountable for the abduction, the press had to create scapegoats so naturally that honour fell upon the Gardai .

Certainly, he was no wiser now than he had ever been and the pressure from his superiors wasn't making it easy. Even the Taoiseach and other members of the government had joined the chorus of disapproval but no-one, it seemed, had come up with a plausible explanation or solution to the mystery or what form the next move should take.

And now tonight's latest irritation. Dennis Ahearne's fuzzy-haired wife appearing on The Late, Late Show bemoaning the inadequacies of the police and stating that she and her son were bringing her husband home from 'that place in Clare' as the 'so-called specialists' were not doing much to help him. She also spoke about seeking compensation from the coach company and possibly from the Gardai, although try as he may he couldn't see how she stood a cat's chance in hell with that notion as her husband had been the one driving the coach and therefore the one responsible for its safety.

Downing a slug of Jameson's, he ignored the texts from well-intentioned fellow officers telling him exactly what he had just seen. Did they think he wouldn't have been watching? Dennis Ahearne's condition remained much the same as it had when he first turned up, and as far as Tierney knew, he had offered no more pronouncements since that day when the two dancers had visited.

He gave a groan and kicked off his shoes. The family had gone to bed and the weekend was just beginning. The first weekend he had freed up since the disappearance and he had promised them a film and pizzas and whatever else they wanted to do as they had hardly seen him while his working days and nights had taken him out of the city.

He had now been reminded so sweetly by his wife that the year was almost over and that the so-called season to be jolly would soon be sprinkling its tinsel trail through stores and homes across the world. But it wouldn't be so jolly for those families of the missing dancers and, to be blunt, would be bloody awful for him too if they weren't found by then.

His phone buzzed and he saw that the caller was Gerry Doyle. They had become mates over the last few months, drawn together by their common professional bond and the joint frustration it had produced for both of them.

"Hello there, Gerry. Any news?" He was getting accustomed to using the question as a form of greeting but it was beginning to sound hollow and rhetorical.

His friend surprised him with his answer. "Joe, have you by any chance seen a copy of this morning's *Boston Herald*?"

"Is this a trick question Gerry? Why would I have seen an American newspaper?"

"I'll copy it and send it through. You should get it in a few minutes. Okay?"

Joe was already on his way to his computer. "Okay. I'll call you back."

Nursing his whisky glass in one hand he switched on the machine with the other and waited for the e-mail attachment to appear. Sure enough, the ping signalled its arrival and Joe

Tierney pushed the mail key to read what his colleague had forwarded.

The newspaper print that the article had been copied from was small so he fiddled around for a while trying to get the font enlarged. What he read produced a combined reaction of surprise and exasperation for under a headline that read 'Could this be the person who solves the mystery of Arcanum?' a photograph of a woman with big hair and lots of jewellery smiled out at him. The article went on to state that Blossom Fayard, a well-known local psychic and Tarot card expert had flown to Ireland to meet with her childhood friend Silas Murphy, the creator of the troupe, in order to solve the strange case of their disappearance. "Although there appear to be very few leads at the moment," Ms. Fayard declared, "I am confident that I can use all the powers at my disposal to get to the bottom of this very unusual occurrence."

Joe Tierney clicked off his computer and returned to the dwindling bottle of whisky. How many had he downed this evening? Two, three? He promised himself this would be the last one as he flopped back on to the sofa wondering how he should handle this latest addition to the puzzle.

Yes, he had been offered so-called psychic investigators in the past. Many had contacted him directly over the years swearing that they could solve murders or find missing persons but he had never had any confidence in their abilities, had been sceptical of their sworn successes and therefore had declined their offers with polite thanks.

But he was running out of options now so should this one be encouraged? Certainly, if she were here in Ireland and working with the dancers he ought to be involved. He would want to know exactly what a psychic investigation entailed in this particular case and how he could stop it getting out of hand if the woman got too carried away. It was a risk that he considered might be worth taking but in so doing he would possibly lose the respect of his peers and scorn could be poured on him publicly.

He found himself thinking of Sherlock Holmes of whom he was a fan. He recalled that his hero had stated that once you have eliminated the impossible then whatever you are left with, however improbable, must be the truth.

His fingers hovered over the keypad of his phone for the merest of seconds then reluctantly he called Silas.

★

CO. CLARE.
1735

It gave him no pleasure standing within the dusty gloom of his barn where the raw odour of sex was all too discernable as were the cries of ecstasy and pain, guaranteed to bring the Devil out of his den.

Mick Gilligan had endured the sounds for more than two hours and had come from the house in the desperate hope that the pair would finally reach some degree of mortal satisfaction, and that Kathleen would attend to the business for which they had agreed her lover had been summoned.

Now at last there was a kind of uneasy quietude. In the welcome light from a full moon, he shifted further towards the ladder of the hay loft, not wanting to be heard but knowing he would have to intervene if they fell asleep up there, for time would wait no longer for a truth that had to be plainly spoken and for the fear of God to take the place of indifference.

Then he heard them. A giggle from her and a phlegmy cough from him followed by a spit and then his voice telling her he had to go.

Mick Gilligan jumped back into the shadows as the boy's tousled head appeared at the entrance to the loft. He saw him angrily bat Kathleen's hand away as she clung to his shirt, begging and crying for him to stay.

Then came the sound of ripping fabric and the boy

turned and swore at her with a venom that caused the farmer to seethe. A brutal tirade towards the woman he had just filled with a fountain of sperm and who already had his seed growing inside her.

Still trying to release himself from her grip, the boy grabbed his jacket and climbed clumsily down the ladder as Mick Gilligan walked out of the darkness and Kathleen scrambled towards them, her blouse hanging unbuttoned and her eyes blazing with fear and uncertainty.

For a moment the boy looked vulnerable, cornered. Then he gave a shrug and tried to move out of the farmer's way. But Gilligan held his ground and being the big man he was found it easy to bar the boy's departure.

He just wanted to reason with him. And yes, plead with him if that's what it took to have him face up to his obligations, for he knew now that Kathleen was in no fit state to persuade or to use her head instead of her heart.

But the young man was having none of it. Sullenly, he raised his fists like a child learning to fight. Leaping up and down on the spot as though he was performing some fiendish dance he lashed out with his left and then with his right, taking Gilligan by surprise by punching him squarely in the jaw before trying to make his escape.

Gilligan stood for a moment blinking the dizziness from his eyes then raced after him, the fierce anger that had been brewing inside for weeks now risen to boiling point. Catching up with him just outside the house he grabbed him from behind by the scruff of his neck, shaking him with a fury and a strength he had not realised until then he could ever have possessed.

The boy then started to blubber and plead for mercy as Gilligan marched him back into the barn determined to try and knock some sense into his vain and vacuous head, but before he could draw breath and as unexpected as a thunderclap on a summer's day, he felt the heavy thud of a large object strike the back of his head and was given no choice but to fall to the ground when it struck again, this time against his shins, sending an excrutiating pain soaring through every nerve in his body.

From his position on the hay-strewn floor he stared up at Kathleen Dooley's crazed features. She had thrown the broom aside and was now running to the boy covering him in kisses and enquiring if he were safe.

Mick Gilligan knew that he wasn't seriously injured but he was pretty badly hurt and needed aid. Stretching out his hand towards her for assistance, this time he was kicked back by the boy who laughed in a somewhat hysterical manner at his helplessness while trying to disentangle himself from Kathleen's cloying grasp.

What happened next was immediate and irrevocable. A dark shape loomed in the doorway then leapt like an uncoiled spring directly in Kathleen Dooley's direction.

The giant black dog's eyes were blazing, its jowls curled back over yellow teeth as the boy was knocked flying out of the way of its intended victim.

Mick Gilligan could only yell at the dog and watch in horror from his inert position on the ground. He realised that although Thomas Dooley had given the dog a name he had never known it and to his dismay knew that it would do no good anyway. The animal was determined and focused on the terrified young woman who had run into the corner of the barn and tried to hide behind a pile of hemp sacks.

Snarling furiously, the dog dug away at the sacks, then hurled its weight against her, pinning her to the wall. Oblivious to her screams it tore at her throat as Gilligan continued shouting until he was hoarse and struggled to crawl across the barn towards her. The boy stared at the horrific scene then vomited as a torrent of blood poured from Kathleen's wounds and she uttered one last chilling gurgle before shuddering into silence.

Mick Gilligan was unsure how much time had elapsed since the dog had completed its grisly task, but then watched with astonishment as it ran to his side, wagging its tail in a desire to be rewarded for its efforts.

As the minutes passed, he noticed that the boy was still there, sick and paralysed by his fear of the dog. He raised his head and saw a light bobbing its way towards the doorway and to his great relief his son ran across to him holding a lantern in one hand and a shot gun in the other.

Taking in the scene at a glance, his son embraced him and checked his injuries then walked over to Kathleen Dooley's body and nodded grimly towards Gilligan to confirm that she was indeed dead.

It was then the young Dance Master found his voice, screaming at Gilligan's son to shoot the dog.

"Kill sé. Kill sé."

The farmer's son looked towards the frightened young man who had brought much hope but also such a degree of tragedy to their townland. He gazed upon his pink and white complexion and pearly teeth with sorrow wondering how God could be so unfair to choose a knave for beauty and neglect a true and honest heart like his own.

The curse that the old Dance Master had laid upon them all was only unfolding its dark magic because of his actions and his alone. This intolerable state of affairs was destined to end somehow and over the last few months he had seen his strong father sapped of his precious energy in his endeavours to return the community to some sort of order. Anxiety saps energy, so does antagonism and young Gilligan had little time for either or for watching his father's ever-growing sense of emptiness and physical decline.

Laying aside the lantern, he slowly raised the gun and pointed it at the black dog who fixed him with its golden eyes and gave a low howl.

If the old woman had been present she would have told him that he was aiding her in her quest to complete the cycle. The symbols of the Tarot resonating with real life events and therefore connecting with each other.

The Lovers, the Magician, the Fool, the Hanged Man, Death. It didn't take a wise sage to work out that these cards of the Major Arcana were revealing and predicting the future.

Gilligan's son then pulled the catch on the gun releasing the trigger and at the same time as he heard his father calling for him to stop aimed cleanly at his target shooting the boy between his wide blue eyes.

The deafening shot echoed into the distance of a moist, moon-filled night and the smoke from the black powder rose and then dispersed inside the now hushed barn. Father, son and black dog sat in contemplation as another symbol was subtracted from the pack. Justice.

★

Blossom woke up in Clodagh's flat in Dublin on Monday morning still feeling bad about the newspaper article from her home city which had caught the attention of the Gardai and now seemed to be fairly common knowledge in Ireland.

She had explained to Silas that she had not been asked to give any interviews before leaving the U.S. but while the case was being covered quite extensively in Boston and because she was semi famous there because of her sex change, she had nonetheless been taken by surprise at the airport when a reporter who had found out that they were friends had thrown questions at her regarding her trip.

Silas had been magnanimous in his dismissal of her indiscretion and they had enjoyed a pleasantly relaxed Sunday, driving to Clodagh's parents for lunch where Blossom had appreciated the warm normality of a family atmosphere and, even though the mystery was obviously still the main topic of conversation, it was good for them all to put their feet up, laugh and talk about other less serious matters like the weather, unreliable automobiles and home improvements.

Silas had returned to his apartment last night for the first time in weeks, while Clodagh decided to stay in Donnybrook, giving Blossom her keys and suggesting that she stayed in her place whilst checking it over for any problems that might have arisen while she had been away.

Inside the bright, tidy flat, Blossom studied the numerous

framed certificates and prizes that Clodagh and her friend Sinead had acquired from years of dancing as well as several photographs of the troupe including one in which they were wearing their colourful Tarot costumes. She also noticed a fair amount of religious paraphernalia on the mantelpiece which, although it was not that surprising as they were both Irish Catholic girls, did give her pause for thought.

She had recognized as soon as she met Clodagh that she was a kindred spirit, deeply sensitive to elements not just confined to this worldly plane and Blossom was glad that she was able to enlighten the girl about her seven senses which in part had been awakened through the spirit of the dance. It was clear that the dancer had been aware for some time that there was something different about her and needed to be reassured that she was not delusional and that any gifts she was blessed with should be encouraged.

This morning they had been called to a meeting with Superintendent Joe Tierney whom she had heard about from Silas and whom it looked as though she would have to convince to keep an open mind if they were to work together. He sounded like a nice guy, but after all he was a cop and used to dealing in hard evidence.

At Gardai Headquarters where they met he shook her hand firmly and she was interested to observe that he didn't show any outward signs of being bothered by the fact that she had once been a man. That, to Blossom, was a big plus in his favour and she felt that they could both enter the meeting without any feelings of awkwardness which might distract from the difficult conversation that was no doubt to come.

As she anticipated, he opened the meeting in a way that was both cautious and sceptical.

"Ms. Fayard, tell me what you think you can bring to this case that the Gardai, the MPB and the National Bureau of Criminal Investigation can't?"

Silas and Clodagh both glanced at Blossom, awaiting her response.

Blossom leaned back in her chair with an expression

of calm confidence. "Because, Superintendent, you are all looking in the wrong direction."

"Enlighten me." Joe Tierney said wearily.

Blossom smiled to herself, thinking that might take somewhat longer than the time they had put aside today.

"Superintendent, I am certain that you and your colleagues do not consider this to be a straightforward case of kidnapping or abduction, because by now, three months on, someone would have been in touch. I also know, as I'm sure you do, that it is almost impossible to hide twenty-five people and a large vehicle without somebody somewhere noticing and that in an age of such advanced technology, there has been no cell phone communication from them. Therefore, we have to look at the clues thrown up by something outside of our normal sphere of understanding. Silas has asked me to be involved because I believe more than ever, now that I am here in your beautiful country, that this is a paranormal disappearance and that I will soon begin to understand why it happened and how it can be solved."

"What clues are you referring to?"

Blossom knew she would have to confess to what Silas had told her. "I do know that the driver has seen something, been somewhere if you like, which has so terrified him that he is unable to remember or speak clearly about the experience. This would tie in with a natural reaction that some people have when witnessing a supernatural phenomena of some magnitude. What I am trying to work out from this particular clue is why he is the one to return from wherever he has been and the others haven't."

"Can you tell me, in layman's language so that I can understand, just where you think this...mythical place might be?"

Blossom shook her silky dark hair. "It's not a place as such. It's another dimension. Perhaps another time in another dimension. Have you read about anything like this and does it make any sense at all?"

Joe Tierney gave a deep sigh and began doodling on a pad with his pen.

"Not really. What are the other clues?"

Blossom decided not to explain about their recent experience near the lake. This guy could only absorb so much and she would present that later if it became relevant. "One other clue, Superintendent." She held out her hand to Clodagh who passed her the card. "Clodagh and Silas discovered this near the spot where the driver was found. It's a Tarot card and I believe someone is trying to tell them something significant."

Joe Tierney took the card which Blossom handed to him and flipped it over in his hand. "I'm sorry, Ms. Fayard, I can't see why you would think that a card that could have just been dropped has anything to do with the disappearance."

Blossom retained her patience, keeping her voice steady. "Because, Superintendent, it's a Tarot card. Not just any card, but from a pack which not only is linked to divinatory practices but has been described as the universal key to all religions. The Tarot offers a way to personally connect with a variety of myths and visions. And surely you don't regard it as coincidence that the name of the missing troupe is Arcanum and the dance that gave them that name was based on these cards?"

The detective examined the card again then raised his eyes, surveying all three of them doubtfully.

"As you say, Ms. Fayard, this for me is certainly outside the sphere of normal understanding. I'm sorry but I just cannot see how I can persuade my superiors to spend time and resources on something so…so frankly unbelievable."

Blossom looked quickly at Silas and Clodagh. "Superintendent, I do not want your money. I would only call on your time and assistance if I need to gain access to places or people who might be able to help me. I know it's all very difficult to take on board and I thank you for your time this morning."

She rose from her chair and Joe Tierney gestured to her

to remain seated. "What I'm saying Ms. Fayard, all of you, is that I will continue to pursue what I see as normal lines of enquiry, credible theories, regarding missing persons. I won't prevent you from conducting your own extraordinary investigations as long as they do not in any way prevent my officers from doing their job. Oh, and although I can't stop you talking to the press, I would much rather you didn't encourage them otherwise it will turn into more of a circus than it already is. Do I make myself clear?"

"Clear as a bell." Blossom told him, raising her hand to her forehead in a salute and drawing relieved laughter from the others. "And I suppose we say now that we'll be in touch, isn't that how we part?"

Joe Tierney walked round from behind his desk to once again shake her hand. "Yes, Ms. Fayard. That's how we part."

★

They arrived back in Ennis earlier than expected and while Silas and Blossom returned to the hotel, Clodagh decided to go straight to the theatre to warm up before the show that evening.

She could hear music and the clicking of dance shoes coming from the stage and, as she entered the auditorium saw that the group from Lighthouse were rehearsing a new routine.

Erin was standing in the front row fiercely calling out directions so Clodagh chose a seat further away so that she could watch them for a while before slipping into her woollen tights and performing her exercises backstage.

Although the two leads still did not possess the chemistry which she knew that Erin was looking for, the troupe itself was getting better, stronger and more confident, and Clodagh was once again aware of how much she missed the spirit of camaraderie that working as a team can bring. For a brief moment she allowed her imagination to superimpose the faces of her lost friends over those of the dancers on the stage and, in so doing, felt the all too familiar emotion of bereavement welling up in her eyes and throat.

Swallowing back her tears, she suddenly noticed something happening on the stage which made her sit up and for a moment forget her despair. Was she dreaming or were the boys waving the fake swords and the long laser lights which Arcanum used in their Tarot finale? Then she saw four of the girls entering holding goblets, and another four with small candle lamps shaped in the form of pentacles. Clodagh stood up and moved closer, unable to believe what she was seeing. The dancers were using Arcanum's props and Erin was directing them in what she perceived to be a dance based around the suits of the Tarot.

Clodagh found herself running towards the stage. "Erin, what are you doing?"

The dancers froze while the music tape continued playing. Different music from Arcanum's but not that dissimilar. They looked awkward and apprehensive, sensing that Clodagh was not happy with what she was seeing and some of them wandered off into the wings.

"Alright, guys. Take five." Erin told them and turned to beckon Clodagh to sit beside her. But Clodagh remained standing.

"Erin, you're using our props. What's happening?"

"I was going to say something Clodagh, but you and Silas are always so preoccupied. The props are just sitting there, not being used. I thought I'd base a small routine on the Tarot which you can use as part of your set if you want to. I'm not using Silas's choreography and it seems a shame not to…" She broke off as Clodagh interrupted her angrily.

"Capitalize on it? Is that what you want to do, Erin? Use the loss of our dancers to work your own routine to Silas's idea? To invite publicity? That is shameful, Erin. I'm surprised that you can stoop that low!"

But instead of apologizing, the woman became defensive. "Clodagh, I was going to hire the props from you. Pay you for them. We will supply our own costumes. There's nothing else we are doing that's the least like Silas's vision. It's just a dance, Clodagh. Lighten up."

Clodagh couldn't remember when she had ever felt so angry and hated herself for the negative resentment which sat in her stomach now like a pile of stones.

"I'm asking you as politely as I can, Erin. Please do not proceed with this or I shall have to tell Deirdre we can no longer perform here."

Erin pushed some scripted papers into her briefcase and snapped it shut. "Alright, Clodagh. We'll scrap it for here. But I'm telling you that if your dancers are not found by Christmas, I shall continue working on a Tarot routine for our tour in March. You know you have no legal right to stop someone else doing that routine. And if Lighthouse doesn't do it, you can bet your pants some group of Irish dancers somewhere in the world will soon."

When she had swept out, Clodagh steadied herself and took several deep breaths before moving. Once again, Erin Shaw had set her thinking about the possibility of Arcanum never being found. Was she right? And would someone else steal their idea for the publicity it would attract? The more she thought about it the more likely a scenario it became.

It was a human condition that she struggled to understand. There were always people who would jump on an easy bandwagon however much hurt and distress it could cause to others. And once again, not caring who could hear, she spoke aloud and with resolution into the now quiet theatre. "We're going to find them."

★

CO. CLARE.
1735

The time had come.

The old woman grimaced as the fork lightning zig-zagged

across the ruins of the stone tower, painting yet another card of the Major Arcana. Sheltering from the midnight storm, she had no concept of time. Her fervent incantation had been continuing for what felt like hours, and she knew that if she had read the cards correctly then it would negate the old Master's curse and thereby offer a solution to all of their woes.

Rumour had it that Kathleen Dooley and that rakehell had run off together but she believed otherwise. She had gone to his house and the costume was there as was a bagful of gold coins which he would have rather died than leave behind.

None of that mattered now as she had taken away the costume and he would never get to wear it again. He hadn't been evil, just weak and immoral, a young man intent on worldly success, but by paying such scant attention to her late Master's words, he brought discord where there had once been order. And for that, in her eyes, no punishment was too great.

She had seen and lived through the long, cruel years. Years when her Master had risked his life in his desire to bring joy to the people who most deserved it. He had defied that tyrant Cromwell's ban on dancing and had secretly gone about nurturing the great tradition in the face of moral and political adversity, knowing that Irish dance embraced the sufferings of an ancient people.

Now as she waited for their salvation, for the first time she felt fear. The words she repeated were of an arcane language learned from her Master and as the thunder rumbled in the distance she noticed the pearly grey mist swirling ahead of her and her whispered chanting ceased as the sound of the thunder became louder and closer. A sound like she had never heard before, almost deafening and causing her to back away, raising her arms in a defensive gesture, unsure of what was coming towards her through the murky veil.

There was a smell too. It blew through the now hot air reminding her of goose fat or strong rapeseed.

Then the beast showed itself and the old woman cowered

in fright. In an instant she realised that she might have taken her occult practices too far and summoned up a dark demon as warned by those who feared the Trionfi. Others in the village would be falling on their knees and making the sign of the cross but she only believed in the ancient wisdom and was sure it would not let her down now at such a crucial time.

But the eyes. There seemed to be four of them, two large and two smaller each side of its sleek, black head, and they were burning white. Their glare lit up the immediate landscape and outlined the trees in the infinite forest space beyond in a blaze of power and which she knew beyond doubt was the work of supernatural forces.

Then a fraction of silence before the lights were extinguished and darkness surrounded her once more. Darkness in which this monster lurked. Was it going to seek her out and kill her? She remained rigid until a sound reached her ears which allowed her petrified body to relax for a brief moment. It was the sound of human voices. Many voices chattering against each other. Then a light blinked above her and the old woman let out a gasp of wonder as she saw a group of human beings staring out of the monster and in her direction.

She jumped as the eyes lit up again, blinding her vision, and above the voices she heard a creaking sound followed by a bang and into the light walked the figure of a man.

She stood her ground as he lurched towards her, dragging his feet in the thick mud and she saw that there were purple spots on a face contorted with confusion and fury.

He began to speak and she struggled to understand as his words sliced through the ether. "Where the feck are we? Who are you?"

The old woman drew her shawl tighter around her in apprehension, as the man, dressed in a strange black suit, came closer.

"I said where are we? Am I near Ennis?"

Her fear of the now silent monster was slowly diminishing. She understood the name of the town the man spoke of and nodded her head vigorously, pointing behind her into the dark, tree-filled distance.

The man was not appeased. "Where's the road you idiot? Where's the Ennis road?"

"Stop that!"

The old woman blinked into the light wondering who had called out and as curiosity and courage began to replace fear, moved slowly forward while the silhouette of a tall young man climbed out of the monster. Taking cautious steps towards him she was halted once again in her tracks by the sight of another young person, then another and another following him out of the large black devil.

They were all so pretty. Young men and women, who although dressed in the most ugly of garments, filed out and walked towards her in an unthreatening manner.

The voice came again. "I said, stop that! Stop bullying that old woman."

She tried to make out the odd word or two of English that she was hearing now and might have heard spoken over the years, but as her Master had only used old Irish and Latin, it was an impossible task. She would have to believe her eyes and her instincts and something was telling her that these young people were to be trusted.

The man mumbled something and watched as the group surrounded her. Voices swam in her ears speaking words that she could not understand and she found herself grinning. There was absolutely nothing to fear, of that she was sure.

"Can you tell the driver how to get back onto the road?"

"Is there somewhere we can get a better signal? Our phone's aren't picking up."

"Is there anyone else who can help us?"

And then – "An bhfuil Gaeilge agat, a seanbhean?" ("Do you speak Irish, old woman?")

The young man in a woollen hat with the soft brown eyes who had been the first to appear was speaking in an accent which she could just about grasp. Nodding, she moved to take his hand and he smiled at her kindly.

"Mise Terry." He told her, pointing to his chest and indicating his name.

"Terry." She lisped, still holding on to his hand. And then buoyed on by the excitement of the night's events and longing to know if her incantation had really worked, she uttered the only English words that she could speak and the only ones that really mattered now. "Dance Master?"

★

It was a subdued threesome that returned from the Lough that afternoon. They had hoped that by visiting the same spot at around the same time, they might have once again encountered a vision of the past but it was not to be. No silver mist, no sound of silence and no dislocation proved a disappointment and after they had tucked into large bowls of fresh seafood broth at the local pub, Blossom told them that she wanted to go to the library in order to do some further research on the area.

Finding a quiet corner inside the high ceilinged, wood panelled room she opened her lap top and clicked on to the search engine. Although this was not the first time she had studied the local history, she was once again struck by the terrible injustices the local people had suffered through the great famine, the cholera epidemic and of course the barbarous Penal laws which had persecuted those who wished to follow their Catholic religion and prevented them from holding any form of government office or joining the fighting forces.

Blossom gazed out of the window at the gathering dusk. Children coming out of school were pulling on their mothers' hands, laughing and skipping happily along with not a care in the world. Certainly with no thought of what had happened in times gone by or what was to come. Only considering the moment.

Blossom stretched and returned to her screen, knowing that she was going to uncover a plethora of information but nonetheless typed 'Myths and Legends in County Clare' into the search engine. As anticipated, hundreds of titles confronted her and she scrolled down passing over the obvious. Countless manifestations in numerous castles, faery folk and banshees, battle-weary fighters and animals which consisted mainly of dogs, cats and horses all of which were black, as well as giant badgers and mad hares.

She wasn't sure what she was looking for but knew that they desperately needed more clues than the tenuous ones they had so far. It would help if she was able to pin point the time-slip into a particular period but what they had witnessed could have been set in any century prior to the early nineteenth when the churches in the town had been built.

Blossom was obviously no sceptic but even she had to suspend belief at some of the experiences that were so colourfully described and when, by complete mistake, she hit on the subject of U.F.O's, the amount of coverage the phenomena excited was seen to be enormous.

Guiltily aware that she was wasting precious time, she scrolled through the country's many eye witness reports from the first sighting of flying saucers to be documented in Kerry in 1947 up to the present day over The Burren where the very bones of Ireland's landscape seem to break through its skin.

A yellow pool of light flooded through the library for which she was grateful as her eyes were tiring from the intense mixture of concentration and frustration. Now she needed to dig out some of the dusty government files and parish records from as far back as they had been catalogued, most of which were simply showing the prominent families who had owned land in the immediate areas, together with lists of local traders, births and deaths.

Strangely enough, the U.F.O information was also present beneath some of these historic headings. Blossom learned that the Irish had long believed in Tuatha De Danaan, which translated into Ancient Aliens, travelling in what they called demonships and first recorded as early as around 456 AD.

She noted that the late, great poet Seamus Heaney had paid tribute to the monks of Clonmacnoise, just a stone's throw away from where she was sitting now and who had recorded their experience of seeing such a ship coming down from the sky whilst they were at prayer. This close encounter had been chronicled in AD 1211.

Fascinating as all this was, Blossom was still no nearer to finding out more about the time-slip which they had experienced and into which she was convinced the dancers had been drawn. Scrolling down the snippets of information from the twelfth century to the eighteenth, she read then re-read a few lines which began to stimulate her interest.

'In the very pleasant hamlet of Rossroe' – she noted that there was a double 's' in the name then – 'in the Barony of Tutlagh, parish of Kilmurry, in 1735, there were reports of a godless apparition found in a field which had caused consternation among the clergy and other dignitaries. The High Sheriff of Clare himself had been called to examine the strange black object but no-one was able to explain its presence or the materials from which it had been constructed.'

Blossom's heart began to race and it seemed as though she had been allowed to open a door just wide enough to see shadows but not enough to discern the forms that cast them.

If the segment from the historic catalogue she had just unearthed described the place and the year of their time dislocation and the 'godless apparition' was indeed the coach, then she was near and yet still so far from a conclusion. For although those vital components were essential to their search, she would now need to discover why it had been chosen to cross the path of time and how on earth the people carried in it could be returned.

★

CO. CLARE.
1735

Terry Riley felt like an alien. The only member of the group to have been wearing a watch and to have brought with him a pen and a note pad. Not that a watch was going to make a blind bit of difference, for like the engine of the coach, their phones and their tablets, it had stopped the minute they had arrived in this weird place with its similarly weird inhabitants.

Since the moment of their first encounter with the old woman near the castle, things had gone from the absurd to the surreal and now today to the more frightening as the enormity of their capture, as it could now be described, had finally hit home. It seemed that he, in his capacity as tour manager and being the only one to speak passable Irish, had been firmly designated as leader in a situation which none of them had been able to grasp or work out how to overcome.

That first night, although nerve-wracking, had been looked on as a bit of an adventure. One of those unexpected happenings that can occur then laughed about at some later time. The coach had become lost in a blanket of fog then juddered to a halt in some backward village that none of them had recognised. Dragging their wheelie cases through the mud, they had been led by the woman to the largest of three barns that stood next to a thatched farm-house. Once inside the barn they had been given milk, bread and cheese by the farmer and his wife and son who seemed very hospitable, if peculiar in their dress, speech and manner.

It was made clear to them that they would have to sleep there and would not be able to get to Ennis that night. The farmer had no idea what they were talking about when they held out their phones and chargers and there was no visible electricity anywhere inside or outside of the barn.

Their hosts also seemed mesmerised by the way they were dressed and the toothpaste and shampoo that they used before settling down for the night. The girls in particular had not been happy about washing in cold water from an outside well nor about the two rough towels that had been brought out to share between twenty-five people. They were also deeply embarrassed and shamed by squatting behind trees and bushes to perform their toilet functions.

But whereas they had accepted these inevitabilities as temporary hardships, the driver had not. Refusing to leave the coach, he had slept the night there and forewent the offer of food. He would 'get the feckin' ting working,' he said, but of course he hadn't and stormed into the barn the next day demanding to be driven to the nearest fuel station. This had once more been met with what appeared to be genuine bewilderment and the driver had become apoplectic with rage until handed a jug of porter which he drank thirstily before slipping into a drunken stupor.

Terry looked around at his friends huddled together in the straw, lit only by one solitary lantern. Sinead and Michael were deep in whispered conversation, others were praying and a few of the girls had been crying again, their faces as pale and damp as Victorian heroines, and although the boys were trying to be strong for them, he knew that beneath the bravado lay genuine terror and uncertainty of what was to come. "We'll miss the show" had now been poignantly replaced by childlike pleas of "I want to go home," from each and every one of them.

He had tried to tick off the days as best he could from the time they arrived and realised to his dismay that it had been roughly eight weeks. It was also not hard to notice the sharp change from autumn to winter while dozens of brittle leaves floated around the yard in an air laced with frost.

The farmer who was called Mick had told them that they could not leave until the time was right and if they did he insisted somewhat ridiculously that they would be captured by the authorities and thrown into gaol. The man seemed so convinced of this, that despite their protests, Terry felt in his bones it might just be a possibility and they had obediently only left the barn in the mornings and evenings to wash and to collect drinking water, fiercely guarded over by a large black dog who he knew would not hesitate in bringing them down if they tried to make a run for it. One or two had ventured further, but soon returned, terrified by the dog, the foul weather and not having the faintest idea in which direction they were heading.

Only the driver had fled after trying to attack the farmer and his son. The dog had gone for his leg clenching it between its powerful jaws while the man had screamed like a banshee trying to tear himself free. The farmer had then called off his dog and the driver limped away into the dense countryside, never to return.

Before he had become aware that they were being held prisoners, Terry had tried to make sense of what the old woman was talking about through her language of stressed syllables and consonant changes. He had explained to her that he was not a dance master and if she meant choreographer, then Silas Murphy was not travelling with them. This had upset her greatly and she had hunched herself into a corner of the barn where she produced a small velvet bag from her petticoats, rocking to and fro and muttering words that he was unable to decipher. He had tried to comfort her but she had pushed him away.

The following day she was gone. Terry had asked the farmer who she was and why she was enquiring about a dance master, but the farmer was not talking. Terry could sense however that he and his family were anxious to find her and was pretty sure that they were taking it in turns to search when the cart was driven out of the farm at daybreak every morning.

He turned his head sharply as another scream from one of the girls announced the familiar visitation of a mouse or a rat scurrying across their bodies as they tried to rest. Most days they had spent limbering up and exercising in order to keep supple, aware that as precision dancers they had to retain as much training as possible. It was as natural a function for them as drawing breath, and Terry was filled with admiration at their dedication and discipline, knowing that it also helped keep them motivated and optimistic.

The biggest mystery of all was why nobody had yet found them. They had gone off the road only a few kilometres from Ennis so how in God's name could it be taking so long? He could only imagine how worried Silas and Clodagh would be, not to mention their families and loved ones, and it was impossible to believe that the Garda hadn't been alerted and mounted a search operation.

This morning they had put their heads together for yet another group discussion and decided that they would pool their financial resources in an attempt to bribe the farmer to at least drive them to the nearest town in his horse and cart. Terry would also ask him for a map of the area as they were desperate to know where precisely they were.

He collected a total of one hundred and twenty euros and when Mick appeared with their now regular breakfast of a large pot of lumpy porridge with creamy milk straight from the cow, a couple of wooden spoons and something vile which passed for coffee, Terry knew that they could wait no longer to make a serious effort to escape.

But once again their plans were to be thwarted. As Terry pushed the coins and notes into the farmer's hand, he saw him gaze at them in total incomprehension.

"It's yours." Terry told him. "Please get us out of here now."

The man shook his head and tried to return the money. Some of it fell onto the ground and as Terry bent to retrieve it, he heard Sinead cry out.

"What do you want from us? What do we have to do to get you to let us go?"

The others circled round to comfort her as Terry squared up to the farmer who was roughly the same height although of a much bigger gait. "Okay, I get it. You don't want our money. That's grand. Can you please get us a map? I'd like to know where we are and we'll take our chances on finding our way."

That was when things began to get even weirder. Mick Gilligan then put his hand into the pocket of his shapeless, stained trousers and pulled out some coins which he thrust under Terry's nose. "Money!" He said loudly, his tone matching Terry's in the attempt to communicate. "See! Our money."

Terry took the coins as the others crowded around him. They were made of heavy copper and on one side there was a woman playing a harp and on the other the head of another woman with a fleshy neck and long hair.

"Who's this?" Terry asked.

Mick Gilligan shook his head in confusion, pointing at the coins. "It's herself. Mary."

"Mary? Mary who?"

"The bloody Queen, that's who. Dead now."

Terry didn't turn when he heard the others laughing nervously behind him. Looking closer at the coins he saw to his amazement that the writing around the edge read 'Hibernia. 1722.' Handing them back to the farmer, he asked quietly.

"Mick. What year do you think this is?"

The farmer rubbed his ruddy cheek, rocked slightly on his large boots and turned to address them all. "It be the start of November. 1735."

★

You'd have thought that as a born and bred Catholic he would have experienced some degree of guilt during his thirty-two years of life on the planet, but Silas never knew what a burden it could be until today. An accusing, stifling weight that rested on his head and shoulders and which could possibly be alleviated by the power of prayer or a visit to the confessional, but that was a path he had chosen not to follow.

Guilt for not travelling with them on the coach then guilt for not having found them, and now this afternoon, more guilt in declining to join Blossom and Clodagh, who had formed a very special bond, on their daily pilgrimage to the Lough, for try as he may he could not ignore the disturbing vision of his two dearest friends being swallowed up by the past and lost to him forever.

But he had so badly needed time for himself. Time to reflect on just where they were now in the light of Blossom's remarkable discovery at the library and time to try and work out his future if the worse case scenario meant that the dancers were never coming back.

If it had been anyone but Blossom who had offered up the presence of the coach appearing in early eighteenth century archive material, he would have dismissed it as fantasy. But then he had witnessed so many unexplainable events in the last couple of months that nothing could be that easily dismissed and it had been Blossom who had taught him that coincidences didn't exist, contending that thoughts or events that shared some common meaning were attracted to each other like magnets without a known causal relationship.

The theatre for once was empty. Perfect for self-reflection but on a more pragmatic level also perfect for trying out a new pair of shoes which he had ordered weeks ago and which he now slipped on, testing the hi-tech heels for superior sound and also for their lightness and flexibility essential to the jig he was performing nightly. The shoes were his support system, for if the size varied one centimetre it could throw his balance askew, but unlike the old ones which meant wearing in the soles against the consistency of the stage floors over a period of time, these split-soled new ones enabled him to control the technique of his exacting spins and turns almost immediately.

The backstage area carried the usual rancid, though evocative scent of greasepaint and sweat within a space which was never entirely light nor dark and Silas decided to first work his steps there in front of the large gilt-framed mirror spotted with age and which leant at an angle against the rough brick wall.

He had learned by now which movements were the most fulfilling and which were defiantly more dangerous. Through years of experience he had employed cleverly worked out short cuts and pain saving devices so knew how much breath was needed in order to pace himself.

The shoes were comfortable, that was a good sign, and for some bleak reason he was suddenly reminded of Nijinsky who was presumed to have gone insane when working out the choreography to "Sacre." Some blamed the savagery of the music and in keeping to its spirit he had danced without shoes, using flat pounding rhythms with his bare feet. Others had suggested that it was an over-reach on his part, a will for perfection which could not be humanly achieved, not even by the fabulous Nijinsky.

Now as he slowed down, preparing to continue his moves on the stage, Silas was diverted by what seemed to be a slight change in the tincture of the dark silvery glass of the mirror, which appeared to be draining everything it reflected of its colour.

At first he thought that someone must have opened one of the fire doors causing a draught that had filtered moisture onto the glass, and hoped that it wasn't Erin. He hadn't spoken to the choreographer since Clodagh had told him that she had been using their props for a Tarot routine, as he didn't have the will or the energy to get into an argument with the woman.

Pausing to listen for footsteps, he heard nothing and returned his attention towards the mirror. Now, his heartbeat accelerated, as he was sure he could see some sort of transformation occurring within the vaporous glass. He was reminded of that day by the Lough when they had unwittingly moved back in time and suddenly he realised that someone or something was trying to make contact with him. How different it was now though, for he was on his own and the degree of nervous excitement he was experiencing was made all the more overwhelming by his innate sense of isolation.

What if he got it wrong and interpreted some vital message incorrectly? He looked wildly around as if willing Clodagh and Blossom to appear beside him to offer moral support but there was no-one other than him and his slowly decreasing reflection.

Then it happened. A swirling, cappuccino mist filled the mirror and he strained his eyes to see what lay behind. He was vaguely aware of a seated figure in a strangely shaped tall hat. As the mist cleared, Silas could now make out the face of an old man with white hair and beard and twinkling blue eyes. His right hand was raised as if in blessing and the upper and lower part of his body was swathed in the dark material of a cloak.

Silas recognised the figure immediately. It was one of the Major Triumphs and the design was once again from the Renaissance deck. The Hierophant was a symbol of alliance, captivity and servitude. He was also represented as a teacher who was regarded as the male counterpart of the High Priestess.

Silas held his breath as the figure ceased to be just a painting on a card. Life gradually flickered behind the eyes and the hand that was raised now moved slightly, curving into a beckoning gesture which seemed to summon Silas to join him inside the mirror.

"What do you want?" Silas heard himself demand, but the figure made no sound, simply continuing to beckon with its long fingers before slowly fading from his fevered gaze.

"Don't go!" Silas shouted, but the image had disappeared and the mirror once again produced his own solitary reflection.

He remained motionless, struggling to assimilate what he had just seen and to translate it into some kind of purposeful structure. Blossom had said that she was trying to connect the dots and Silas, now trembling from a mixture of exhilaration and apprehension realised he had received the message that could do just that.

This latest symbol from the Major Arcana had surely

made it clear. The Hierophant calling to him, coupled with Dennis Ahearne's chilling assertion was enough of a sign to announce that in order to get the dancers back from the past, he would have to sacrifice himself.

★

An unexpected red herring surfaced briefly then dived back into the water and headed out to sea. But it made enough of a splash at the time to persuade Joe Tierney that it might just be what he had been praying for.

A letter had been delivered to Dublin headquarters which stated that the writer was holding the coach and its passengers at a location somewhere between Dublin and Ennis and was demanding the sum of two million euros for their safe return. It also claimed that the kidnapper or kidnappers could show the Gardai proof of authenticity.

The few long months of false hopes and alarms, disappointments and conjecture were now something that felt depressingly normal and even the press were slowly and quietly beginning to reduce their copy to brief paragraphs on inside pages while broadcasters were conspicuously silent, proving that stalemate could not be considered news.

Was it possible that the biggest search ever to take place in Europe had lost its momentum and that the media were really that fickle? It was true that neither he nor Gerry Doyle had given any more press conferences because there was no real news to speak of and they didn't want to raise the families' hopes by suggesting that there might be.

There had been so many crank claims, and although it was a time-consuming and tedious process, they were regularly sorted and dismissed. The coach had been spotted in almost every country in the world and the dancers had been seen in Turkish brothels performing with jewels in their navels as well as living like brainwashed zombie members of a religious cult in Arizona.

This particular claim though had demanded attention because just as he was poised to make contact with the writer of the anonymous note through the media, Joe had received a package left at headquarters overnight, which contained a pink mobile phone bearing the initials M.C. and which had belonged to one of the missing dancers, Maureen Connelly.

The last call made on her mobile was on the morning of the disappearance and there was no DNA evident other than the girl's own fingerprints. Texts and messages were all to friends and family and held no indication of what was to come other than the journey to Ennis that night.

Maureen's mother, a sweet-faced divorcee with blonde, poker straight hair, clutched a handkerchief and wept as she examined the phone, clearly not wanting to return it, but he explained that as that they were treating the kidnapper's request seriously it was a necessary piece of evidence. Did she know what Maureen's movements had been that day before going to the theatre and whether she might have left it somewhere?

Mrs. Connelly didn't know. She simply reiterated that her daughter had left the house as usual to go to work and was definitely carrying her mobile with her then. Joe asked the usual questions about boyfriends but was rewarded by a shake of the head and another storm of tears.

Then, on the morning that he was scheduled to attend a meeting with the Criminal Investigation Bureau to discuss what their next move should be and whether to release some of the charity funds that had been promised online, he received a call which confirmed that this lead was dead in the water.

He had left messages for Silas and Clodagh and only Clodagh had returned his call.

Asked whether she knew anything about Maureen's personal life, Clodagh had told him that as far as she was aware, there was no boyfriend.

She then volunteered the information that she had seen

Maureen dropped off at the theatre that evening by her mother's partner Steve and had waved to him as he drove away in his souped-up MGB sports car.

A check was immediately run on the part time actor whom Mrs. Connelly had lived with for about a year, and it transpired that he had three convictions including an indecent assault on a young girl in Limerick four years previously. "Shouldn't we have known this?" Joe asked angrily, believing that routine checks had been ordered on all the families and those immediately connected to them. But everyone he spoke to passed the buck, adding to his continuing sense of deep frustration.

They brought him in and under the detective's aggressive questioning, the smoothly confident thespian finally confessed to having seen Maureen drop her mobile from her bag as she left his car that evening. From playing the cool dude when he first entered the interview room, he then became less than cool, owning up to making the fake ransom demand and obviously considering that misdemeanour far less serious than the suspicion that he might have behaved improperly with the young dancer.

Joe Tierney watched him being led away and had never felt so empty. Clodagh didn't mention how the trio's own investigations were going and he wondered if it was now time to start seriously reviewing Blossom Fayard's suggestion of what she described as 'looking outside the normal sphere of understanding.'

The concern that scorn from his colleagues and superiors would be released upon him suddenly didn't seem like a problem any longer. He would have to open his mind and view paranormal manifestations not as supernatural phenomena but as natural events subject to rational interpretation.

But he was going to need help.

★

He would locate her tonight, of that he was sure. But as Mick Gilligan pulled to a halt beside the bridge and watched his horse's breath hit the freezing air in a cloud of steam, he suddenly wondered if his need for a priest far exceeded his need for the old woman.

The desire for confession was acute and absolute. He had laid two bodies into the ground without Christian burials and even though he hadn't killed them, he felt a heavy responsibility, for he had lured the boy there and used the pregnant Kathleen Dooley as bait.

But priests were hard to come by these days. Outlawed and threatened, they sought refuge where they could find it. In the ruins of desolate abbeys or with any brave soul amongst the peasantry that might take them in and give them food and succour and he knew of none within the immediate vicinity.

In the forefront of his mind also were the strange ones. The men and women who resembled human beings but spoke, dressed and smelt differently. Were they from the stars? Where had the old woman conjured them up from and when would she return them to their rightful place? Mick felt a deep sympathy in his heart for their unhappiness and for their incarceration, but far more towards his neighbours and friends for whom he still fervently wished a future of joy and hope, free from any curse.

He knew that something had gone wrong. The spell or whatever it was that she tried to evoke had somehow, through chance or destiny, failed to produce the chosen mentor within their midst and that was why he had to find her. The situation was worsening and she was now the only lifeline for the townspeople and for those poor souls imprisoned in his barn.

He had visited the home she had shared with her Master

many times over the past few weeks but she had not been there. Now, as he saw candles burning in the windows, he dismounted and banged on the rotting wooden door determined to extract from her an explanation of whatever magic she was spinning.

She looked joyful. That was the first thing he noticed. Unlike the night of the apparition and the visitors, she was wearing an expression of satisfaction which made him both wary and optimistic.

The first thing she did was press two small muslin bags into his hand. Surprised, he pulled the drawstrings to reveal six gold coins in each. He shook his head but she refused to take them from him and gestured towards her Master's rocking chair for him to sit.

"Dos na cuairteoirí!" ("For the visitors!")

He knew where the coins had come from and simply nodded in understanding. Positioning his heavy frame into the chair he noticed that she had laid her cards out on the table and had been consulting them when he had obviously interrupted her.

Grinning, she gathered them up, shuffled them and then offered him to pick one from the pack.

Mick chose a card at random which meant nothing to him. The picture was of a woman in a blindfold balancing two figures on a wheel while another female figure sat at the top of the wheel appearing to be manipulating it. Beneath the wheel was a bearded old man in white on his hands and knees.

He raised his eyebrows questioningly.

"Athrú Fortúne." ("Change of Fortune") She told him.

"Cathain?" ("When?")

"Go ivath" ("Soon.")

Mick sighed and stood up. It was no use pretending to understand because he didn't, and because she was his only hope in unravelling the unholy mess that had been created, he was forced to believe that this time her prophecy would be right. Things would have to change, and for the better.

★

"Come in, Superintendent." It was late morning when Blossom ushered Joe Tierney into her tiny but comfortable hotel suite after he had called her yesterday. Jugs of coffee and tea were on a side-table along with plates of sandwiches and biscuits indicating an atmosphere of normality, which it was anything but.

He greeted the dancers who seemed distracted. Clodagh, in her practice clothes, was curled up on a window seat watching the shadows of a winter's day pass desolately across the room and Silas unable to sit, paced around anxiously, his forehead knotted into a deep frown.

There was no denying that the room was charged and Joe Tierney realised to his discomfort that these three young people were almost certainly in the grip of the occult. It was something so extrinsic to him that he felt as though he had entered an elite members' club, where everyone else knew the rules and where the men's room was, but regarded those who had just dropped in with some mistrust.

Blossom was wearing a peach sweater over black leggings and the colour flattered her tawny skin. It was shaped in a deep V that hung across one shoulder, while the silver jewellery around her neck and wrists glistened and tinkled harmoniously as she moved. Today she wore little make-up, just a touch of peach gloss on her lips and coal black eye-liner.

He had to keep reminding himself that she had once been a man but refused to be blindsided from the seriousness of the circumstances they were here to discuss.

"May I start this meeting by saying how glad we are to see you, Superintendent. I realise how hard it must have been for you to make that call and it is very gratifying to know that you are prepared to open your eyes to all possibilities regarding this case and that maybe we can work together to bring it to some kind of successful conclusion."

Joe acknowledged her welcome with a nod as she continued.

"By agreeing to participate in our quest, you will now find yourself inside an intricate puzzle surrounded by magical, half-understood phenomenon which we are desperately trying to solve. I mentioned last time about the coach having disappeared into another dimension. What I meant by that is that it slipped into a past date in history. We three have experienced it briefly ourselves and can each swear to its authenticity."

"You have?" Joe asked incredulously. "When and where?"

"Up on the hill near the lake." Clodagh volunteered. "We saw the town before it was even a town."

"You asked when we last met to explain to you in simple layman's terms, Superintendent." Blossom continued. "That is what I will try to do. First, think about the fiction you have encountered about time travel, probably as a child. Think "Doctor Who" meets "Back to the Future," but forget the monsters and forget time machines. They don't exist. Think Woody Allen's "Midnight in Paris." She paused, wondering whether he had seen the recent movie.

"Okay…" Joe nodded. "I saw it."

"Good. Well, but now we get serious. This isn't a romantic comedy. When people encounter glimpses of the past or dislocations as we call it, it is most usually accidental. A trigger such as sunlight flickering through trees or a sudden change in light or maybe a strong sense of history of the place you are in at the time, such as the famous case in Versailles…"

This was lost on the detective but he struggled to keep up with her explanation of what may have occurred and tried not to feel as if he was in some parallel universe of his own.

"To cut to the chase, Superintendent, I strongly believe that the disappearance of the coach and the dancers was not an accidental slip into the past. They were drawn into it by a combination of magic using the Tarot cards, and through a desperate need."

"What kind of need?"

Blossom took a sip of coffee and threw a concerned glance at Silas who had buried his head in his hands.

"I have been researching the history of the area quite extensively to try and find some way of explaining both the disappearance and the Tarot messages and I've had to combine instinct with what I've uncovered. I believe that the year they are trapped in is around 1735 in one of the many townlands that existed then. The overwhelming sadness I experienced just before we encountered the time slip ourselves was palpable and I think it has something to do with dancing and dance masters."

She paused for breath as Joe walked towards the table and poured himself a dark trickle of coffee. "What makes you think that?" He asked, his tone flat though not sceptical.

"Because Superintendent...."

He interrupted, deciding to cut formal ties, after all enough barriers were being dismantled today. "Joe. All of you, call me Joe."

Blossom gave a half smile. "Okay, Joe. I was deeply disturbed to read about the Penal Laws that existed in Ireland up until the 19th century. How it affected religious freedom and property, but also, to my amazement, how it banned Irish cultural traditions, with secrecy demanding that Irish dancing was only practiced behind closed doors. Silas and Clodagh had some knowledge of this, but I had no idea."

This was something Joe Tierney was familiar with and he surprised her by offering up his own understanding of those times.

"That's right. Irish dance dates back to traditions in Ireland in the 1500's and is closely tied to our independence and cultural identity. These ancient dances were never formally recorded or documented due to our occupation by the English. But by the 1700's, dance masters appeared in Ireland and were the creators of the Set and Ceili dances. It was still outlawed then, but some areas were more relaxed than others."

Blossom was impressed. "You know your history, Joe. And you're right, it's difficult to find any records of the dances that were practiced then or anything written about dance during those times." She turned to Silas who had finally decided to sit down. "Do you want to take it from here?" She asked him gently.

"Sure." The worried frown had faded slightly and he leaned forward to make his point. "These dance masters were crucial in keeping the tradition alive and they could be very possessive about the areas where they practiced. For instance, when they were unable to continue either through illness or old age, they would personally try and find another dance master that would take over and he would have to be of a similar high standard or woe betide him if he wasn't."

"Woe betide him." Blossom repeated slowly, turning again to look at the detective who was following everything with more attention than she had expected. "Joe, these guys were flamboyant and probably a little crazy to take such forbidden chances in such dark days. What if, say, a revered dance master had not been able to find someone suitable to replace him? I read that in the courts of Renaissance Italy they took their vocation so seriously that a curse could be placed upon a chosen one who didn't step up to the task."

Joe heard himself laugh, then immediately regretted it. "I believe curses were common in those days."

Blossom nodded. "I'm not one hundred per cent certain that this is what's happened. But I know I'm pretty close. Another Tarot contact was made yesterday from the same Trionfi pack. To Silas specifically."

"So, you think...what? That some place from the past wants Silas to go and be their Dance Master?

Blossom moved her chair closer. "What I'm saying is that through the language of the Tarot I have interpreted the message to the best of my ability. The plan from the beginning was to capture Silas because he chose the Tarot as the theme for his choreography, but it was thwarted because he didn't take the coach that night. They then tried to reach out to Clodagh for help in her role of the High Priestess because she is more tuned in psychically. I believe now that the dancers will come back only if Silas crosses into that other dimension."

A pin could have fallen on the carpeted floor and everyone would have heard it. The silence was so intense that nobody felt they could be the first to speak but it was Silas who found his voice and it was broken and emotional.

"I'm so sorry, I just can't. I don't have the courage. I know I should as it's only me in exchange for so many others, but I'm frightened. I can't give up my life to the past. To an unknown future." He stood up and went to face the window, his shoulders heaving as he gulped back tears of anguish.

While Clodagh and Blossom offered him comfort, Joe collected his thoughts as best he could. He was unable to give them any advice and the problem had still not been solved. In fact this morning's exchange had created new ones. Dilemmas of such magnitude that they seemed impossible to face.

"That's it, then." He said dully, crossing the room to replace his cup on the tray. "If your theory is correct then they're never coming back."

With great effort Silas pulled himself together and repeated his regret.

"You don't need to keep saying sorry." Blossom told him. "No-one expects you to make this sacrifice, it's too much to ask. I will have to find a way to communicate with whoever is holding them somehow."

Just as he thought he had heard it all, Joe Tierney was to always remember the time and the place where he witnessed the next words that would change the goalposts yet again.

"I'll go."

Clodagh's voice was strong and determined, hypnotic as the wind whipping up outside the window.

"If they are waiting for a teacher, then I will help them. It might take them a while to accept a woman in the role of Dance Master, but when they see that I can dance and choreograph, it shouldn't be a problem. I'll go."

"No!" Silas cried, rushing towards her. "I can't let that happen."

Clodagh stretched out her hands to keep him back. "You have no choice in the matter, Silas. This is my decision and it feels right for me."

Blossom took a deep breath and rose from her chair. She spoke softly, looking at the girl with admiration and understanding. Yes, of course that was meant to be. How could it be any other way?

"Alright." She said firmly. "Let's make plans."

★

She had visited the church immediately following the meeting and, as she had been doing regularly since staying in Ennis, lit twenty-five candles in the memory of her friends and for their safe return.

Clodagh gazed up at the blue-robed figure of Mary cradling the baby Jesus in her arms and once again envisaged the High Priestess. What was it about the old religions and women? There was no doubt that they were held in the deepest of respect, were powerful emblems of their gender and could exercise control in a fair and moderate fashion. Yet notably, the two most prominent female figures from the Bible, Eve and Mary were, as her dream had suggested, hardly models of female emancipation.

Clodagh knew that she could never abandon her faith but having made the decision to take Silas's place on this vital journey into the unknown, it was as though she were travelling towards some kind of mystical destiny. She had been instructed through a dream to connect with her inner wisdom and everything that had happened in the last few months had been building up to this decision; the Sister's words at the hospital, her sense of being part of a universal whole during her long walk and Blossom's recognition of the freeing up of her spirit through dance.

But she also considered herself a modern day feminist, a

young woman living and working in the twenty-first century who had grown up with a dancer's ferocious discipline and attention to detail. This year, she realised she had been searching for something intangible, a pursuit through which she could exercise her creative talents and also satisfy the cravings of her psyche. If Blossom's theory was correct, then she could aid those who were lost both metaphorically and literally and the sense of achievement that she would experience would be like no other.

That was not to say that she was without fear. The immense excitement of the coming challenges mingled with trepidation flowed through her veins like a fever, for this was no normal adventure. She knew that Blossom would guide her safely towards the path, but the pain she would have to endure before then when leaving her family would be tortuous. Would she ever see them again? Who could say? And how would they ever understand? But while so many things in life were uncertain, hanging on a tenuous thread that could snap at any given moment or bend on any whim of fate, then she would deal with it when the time came by embracing yet another symbol of the Major Arcana. Fortitude.

★

That night their eyes spoke a language which had nothing to do with the story behind the dance. His were burning, pleading with her to change her mind. Hers sympathetic but resolute and while the heels and toes of his new shoes seemed to drive the steps he performed even harder and faster than before, each played out their sweetly sad finale in front of an audience totally unaware of the enormous pressure their two favourite dancers were experiencing.

When it was over, she wanted to go back to the hotel and sleep. He wanted to talk.

"Not tonight, Silas. I'm very tired." She told him, packing up her bag and collecting her jacket and scarf.

He wasn't going to allow her get away with it that easily. "I need to understand Clodagh," he said, blocking her exit towards the dressing-room door. "You must explain to me why you are doing this. Do you really know what you will be giving up if this crazy plan goes ahead?"

She let her bag drop to the floor with a weary shrug. "I'm not stupid, Silas. Nor am I a child. I don't expect you to understand my reasons, but I have no illusions about what I'll be giving up or what I'll be going into. No proper medicine, no electricity, showers, I-pods, burgers, mobiles…the list is endless. Of course I know. But it doesn't matter. None of it matters because twenty-five people will be free and in a way that you could never understand, so will I."

He could only stare at her miserably, still unable to believe she would willingly take herself into the dark, cold past without any of the comforts and essentials she had always taken for granted. It was as if two women inhabited her body, one infected by a powerful sense of urgency to embrace this uncertainty and the other the person he had known for so long, curious, yet grounded and certainly not reckless.

"What about the people who love you, Clodagh? I can accept you don't care about me, but what about your mum and dad. Auntie Peggy?"

"Don't you think that hurts me, the thought of losing all of you? Of course it does. But I can only hope that in time the sadness will fade and you will all continue to remember me lovingly and with joy. Don't forget you told me that whatever path I chose to follow, yours would never be far away."

He hadn't forgotten, but he didn't mean for her to disappear into another century. He knew then that it was useless to try and apply reason to a situation where there was none. He also knew that there was no sense of ego involved. She wasn't playing the heroine and there was no hint of seeking fame or gain in her decision. She genuinely believed that she was doing was the right thing and if he couldn't talk her out of it then no-body could.

He decided as a last resort to try doubt. "And if it doesn't work? After all, it's one hell of a long shot. I really don't think you can change the past. You can only try and change the present and the future, that's always possible, but not the past."

She smiled her gentle smile and kissed him lightly on the cheek, picking up her things again as he allowed her to pass.

"It's already been changed, Silas. And not for the good. So I can only try in my small way to make it work."

★

Joe Tierney wanted to discuss strategy at headquarters and had summoned the three of them to Dublin when he had heard that Blossom had worked out a way forward. He had also given them strict instructions to revert to calling him Superintendent for the purpose of the meeting.

Silas was unsurprised to see Gerry Doyle there but was not expecting the Commissioner plus a representative from the CIB, and realised that this was going to be a pretty high-powered, full on meeting. Obviously, it was such a massive issue that others would have to be involved, but he hoped that Blossom would not be fighting too much scepticism from those on the other side of the desk whose minds would certainly need some persuasion to accept the strangeness of the story so far.

Joe had filled his colleagues and superiors in and to their credit they did not interrupt Blossom but listened intently when she was invited to explain just what was going to happen next.

Silas was so proud of his old friend. Dressed today for the seriousness of the occasion in a black trouser suit with a plain, white silk shirt, she appeared assured and sophisticated. The jewellery, of course was evident, but her hair was drawn back with a coral clip accentuating the cheekbones which he had always remembered Billy having, though since the surgery seemed more pronounced and chiselled.

Clodagh as ever, looked beautiful. Even with no make-up and her long hair tucked inside the high-necked collar of her green sweater, she still seduced his heart into performing a series of double jigs and he tried to control the desire to move his chair closer in order to hold her hand.

He became suddenly aware that Blossom had been speaking for some minutes and he hadn't taken in a word she was saying. Pulling himself back from the wanderings of an overstretched mind, he heard her respond to a question that had come from the Commissioner, a tall man in his fifties in full uniform with dark grey, neatly combed hair.

"How do you see this so-called exchange taking place? You've told us where. We know the characters involved, but just how do you see it happening?"

"We have to take this in stages, gentlemen." Blossom answered. "The first thing I want to do is send a message to the person or persons who has been contacting Silas and Clodagh. They've been communicating through the Tarot so we will begin with leaving a Tarot card in the same place as the other one was found. It will still be the picture of the High Priestess. Only this time it will be one from the best known pack which was created in 1910 and with which those from the other side will not be familiar."

Silas studied the men's faces with interest. Only Joe was following what she was saying with any degree of solid consideration and Silas knew the others were trapped between a rock and a hard place. They had nothing else to go on regarding a case that had captured the world's attention and so were forced to listen and indeed learn.

"But what if someone else picks it up? Someone who isn't from 'the other side?'" The Commissioner asked with the air of superiority his job commanded.

"We will place it down at a very late hour and we'll check that it has gone at sunrise the following day. I am convinced that no-body will be walking around in an unlit, fairly boggy area on a winter's night and notice something as small as a card."

"Surely someone from the Gardai should be there all night?" Gerry Doyle volunteered. "Then we can apprehend whoever it is that's going to take it."

Blossom's expression suddenly changed from pleasantly business-like to sternly adamant. "Absolutely out of the question, Superintendent Doyle. The paranormal doesn't work like that. Nobody must be present once the card is left in the place we specify."

There was a pause until Joe asked the question that had been on the tip of everyone's tongue.

"And what happens if it's not there the following day?"

"If it's not there, we will know that the message has been received. The following night we'll accompany Clodagh to the spot where we experienced the dislocation. I think that as it's not too far from the road then that area should be cordoned off just in case people are still wandering around. If the mist rises and spreads from the lake as it did before then that will be our cue and Clodagh, if she still feels willing and able to commit to this, will pass into it. We can only hope then that the dancers will come out."

Silence and stillness. Just the monotonous click of a giant clock resonating on the wall above Joe's desk. Then a cough, followed by a sound that resembled a laugh, but wasn't quite. The man from the CIB, stocky with enormous eyebrows, then asked for a private meeting.

"Go and get some coffee." Joe told the three of them. "We'll call you back in soon."

They needed to stretch their legs so took their hot drinks outside where Blossom raised a huge yellow umbrella as a faint drizzle crept into the air and Clodagh pulled the collar of her sweater into a hood. Silas realised he couldn't care less about the cold or the rain, for his nerves were jangling like bells calling the faithful to Mass on Christmas day.

"How do you think it's going?" He asked Blossom anxiously.

"Fine." She told him. "Much easier than I expected."

"Why do you think they wanted us out?"

"They needed a reality check. They're still trying to absorb something which they have never in their lives encountered."

"I think Joe's handling it brilliantly." Clodagh. said, stamping from one foot to another in order to keep warm. "He really seems to be in our camp."

"And which camp would that be, I wonder?" Silas didn't mean for it to come out as hard-edged as it had but knew that he couldn't contain his over-sensitivity towards anyone who might support Clodagh's decision. Before the others could react, a young uniformed woman popped her head out of the door and summoned them back into the meeting.

Tierney and Doyle again greeted them pleasantly while the Commissioner and the man from the CIB sat unsmiling behind the long table studying a pile of official looking documents which had not been there before.

Joe cleared his throat. "Blossom, Silas and Clodagh. I am going to have to ask you to sign something for us. This is essential before we are able to proceed with what has just been discussed."

He picked the bunch of collated forms off the desk and handed each of them copies together with three biros.

Silas stared at the heading at the top written in bold capitals. "Official Secrets Act? You can't be serious?"

Blossom, to his amazement tried to quiet him. "It's okay, Silas. Not a problem."

"What do you mean, not a problem? Blossom, you of all people should not be signing this. If what we are about to do is successful, then the world should know about it. You will be able to confirm the existence of things that no-body so far has been able to prove. We should be shouting it from the roof tops."

Blossom remained silent and turned her glance to Joe who was happy to assist.

"Silas, this OSA has come down to us from the Attourney General who has been briefed on what has occurred and what will be occurring. There is no discussion, I'm afraid. You have to sign it or Blossom's careful analysis and work will all be for nothing."

Silas looked desperately to Clodagh but her head was bowed while reading the document.

"And if we get the dancers back? How are you going to shut them up?"

As soon as he asked the question, he realised that it was a lost cause and sat back in his chair feeling defeated. Blossom knew the score. Everybody knew, because this is what happened every time. Whenever, throughout history, an event like this had been uncovered it had to be immediately and irrevocably covered up, even when government ministers, NASA, police and members of the armed forces as well as reliable members of the public had born witness to them. From UFO's to hauntings to time-slips, organised religion and the state must be seen to sustain order and prevent chaos among its citizens. It was the way of the world.

"I see. Bring on the Men in Black, why don't you? Let's go the whole hog!"

Blossom laid a hand on his arm, feeling his frustration and anger, but urging him to sign the form that would never allow him to tell the truth.

"Silas, you're not wrong. Everyone in this room knows that. But if you don't do as they say we will never have a chance to get them back."

"Why not? We can just go ahead without these guys, can't we?"

Joe Tierney shook his head. "I'm afraid that won't work, Silas. Because of what we now know, all three of you would be placed under police surveillance. It could even mean deportation."

Silas stared at him blankly. "You'd actually invent something to make us look like criminals? Or nut cases?" He looked at the others behind the desk who refused to meet his eyes. "Yes, of course you would." He said, suddenly too tired to argue any more as he flipped over the papers on his lap and his pen hovered over the final page. "Okay, here goes my integrity."

"Silas, would you have said that Dwight Eisenhower and Winston Churchill were men of integrity?" Blossom asked, placing her signed copy of the form on the desk.

Silas looked puzzled. "Sure, but what's that got to do…"

"You may not know that in the United Kingdom's national archives are letters and photographs that prove both men covered up a UFO sighting during World War II to avoid mass panic. I have seen one of the letters which describes an incident just off the English coast and involved an Air Force bomber crew which was returning from a photographic mission in Germany or France. It describes the aircraft as being intercepted by an object of unknown origin which matched course and speed with the aircraft for a while, then underwent an extremely rapid acceleration away. It was described as hovering noiselessly and seemed metallic. Sadly, I wasn't allowed access to the photographs."

The top brass exchanged looks which revealed that they had never heard the story.

"Okay." Said Silas. "But our case wouldn't cause mass panic."

The Commissioner spoke up now, in a softer voice than he had used earlier. "The area where all of this paranormal activity has taken place is, as Gerry Doyle will contest, one of outstanding natural beauty. It's managed by the National Heritage and contains not only rare fauna and flora and monoliths of historic significance, but a lake which is popular with those who enjoy fishing and who visit from all over the world. Apart from being an immensely popular tourist destination, many people from our own country holiday there every year and yes, if any of those visitors thought they might get sucked into another dimension and disappear forever, it could cause panic and certainly religious confusion among believers."

"I think the opposite," persisted Silas stubbornly. "I think the tourist trade would flourish. It would be like a religious shrine. A nod to an historic past that crossed the barriers of time in order to overcome adversity. And…" He paused then, giving a choking sigh. "And to remember a woman who offered herself to the unknown in order to save others."

He stood up and reluctantly handed Joe Tierney the signed act of silence.

"Just be very careful with my troupe if we get them back. That's all I ask."

★

CO. CLARE.
1735

A full December moon illuminated an otherwise black night and a lantern was lit once again inside the farmer's barn. On the brick wall behind his head, Terry had noticed the reddish-brown stain of something that looked like faded blood and told himself it had once belonged to some injured animal.

An owl hooted way in the distance, a melancholy sound which transported him back to his childhood home in Cork and only served to make him feel as restless and dislocated as the driftwood carried on a high tide.

Flickering shadows chased the strokes of his pen moving across the note pad as he attempted to use the moon and elementary mathematics to locate the date as best he could and as he tried to settle down for another night of snatched sleep and brooding dreams, hoped that at last freedom was within their reach.

To his frustration and to add to his sense of loneliness, each and every one of the dancers believed they were being held prisoner by a family of backward *culchies,* inbred and ignorant and totally against adjusting their lives to the present day.

Michael had been vehement in this conviction, citing the Amish population in America who refused to move out of the habits and lifestyle of the 18th century, travelling in ramshackle buggies and shunning modern dress and all

142

things electrical as well as speaking in the ancient dialect of their ancestors.

Terry believed differently and couldn't understand their reticence in recognising that they might have become trapped in some kind of time warp. He pointed out what he considered to be clear indications. The money that the Gilligan family was using and Mick's refusal to take euros, no street lights as far as the eye could see, no nearby railway stations and one which he constantly specified, no sound of planes overhead. Even the Amish families couldn't control the propagation of 21st century air travel.

But they had all clung stubbornly to their belief and, he had noted, become more religiously fervent, spending almost as much time in whispered worship during the day as exercising and stretching their noticeably thinner bodies.

And yet, he couldn't really blame them. Everything that had happened was so difficult to accept that adding another layer of uncertainty to their already traumatised lives might be a step too far.

That was why when Mick Gilligan entered the barn earlier that evening to distribute their supper, Terry greeted his words with caution while experiencing heart-stopping excitement.

"You'll be off soon." The farmer had stated gruffly as he placed a large tureen full of thick vegetable soup on the sturdy table that had been erected since their arrival, accompanied by the regular duo of wooden spoons.

"What? When?" The dancers jumped up as if in a choreographed routine and gathered round him. "Has someone come for us?"

Terry once again took charge and asked what seemed like the obvious question. "How are we going to get back Mick? Has the coach been fixed?"

But Mick Gilligan's eyes glazed over and he simply shook his head, repeating the words. "Off soon."

His parting gesture was to hand Terry two small items which he insisted he shared around. This he demonstrated by expanding his arms and sweeping them in a circle indicating that they were all the recipients of his gift.

When he had left, Terry untied the strings that held the muslin bags and showed the others what was inside. Twelve fine gold coins that felt light in the palm of his hand and were engraved with dates that ranged between 1636 and 1647.

"What do we do with them?" asked one of the dancers in bewilderment.

"Are they real gold?" enquired another.

Terry nodded. "I'm pretty sure they are and one thing's for certain. If we ever get out of here, these will provide a nice little nest egg for our future."

This was enough to occupy their thoughts for the rest of the night and the few encouraging words that Mick had left behind meant they could sleep a little easier in their makeshift beds. At least they were now aware that nobody appeared to want to harm them and that it was only through a seemingly endless waiting game that they would be rewarded with their freedom and the chance to be home for Christmas.

They're like children, Terry thought as he watched the hope on their faces, apparent even in sleep. The spectre of their spirits having been raised only to be dashed was too cruel to contemplate and for all of them the following day would either be one of joy or immense disappointment.

★

The card had gone.

Blossom studied the two detectives' faces and saw bare incredulity combined with a primal fear. She watched them separate, moving further away from where it had been left, their torches beaming in the dull dawn light, almost willing it to re-appear and return their stressful lives to the everyday normality to which they were accustomed.

She glanced across at Silas who was staring at the ground with despondent resignation and once again felt so much empathy for where he was right now. She knew he loved

Clodagh with the kind of love that was only ever fated to be unrequited and his suffering was heightened by the reality of what was to happen next in the extraordinary chain of events that were taking their inevitable course.

Clodagh had not come. After the show last night she had returned to Dublin to somehow try and explain to her family that she may be going on a journey and that they would not see her for a while. Blossom wondered how on earth she would handle it. The countless amenities of parting would not be called upon in this context, for true honesty would have to be concealed and she knew how hard that would be for Clodagh of all people.

What would happen tonight was still uncertain. So many elements had to come together to co-ordinate the plan and she knew that it would not simply be a small group of people other than herself, Silas and Clodagh involved in the operation. How many others and just who they might be, remained to be seen, but they would all be instructed to group at midnight in the spot where the time-dislocation had taken place.

She moved towards him and touched his arm, realising there was nothing she could say to ease his pain except "Perhaps it won't happen?" But they both knew that the cards had spoken, affirming in true Tarot fashion the value of imagination, suffering and the sacred aspect of experience through a possible personal journey.

★

CO. CLARE.
1735

The old woman was finding it difficult to tear her eyes away from the brightly painted card and clutched it to her bosom once again, her waxen features unexpectedly stung with the bloom of ripe apples, for this was the sign she had been waiting for.

At first she wasn't sure that it was indeed Herself. The blue was so vivid and the pillars and fruit surrounding the throne hinted of a Biblical significance, as did the book containing the universal knowledge resting on her lap, but the more she looked, the more she became convinced that this was HER High Priestess, the fount of all knowledge, reliable, sincere and revered.

From whence it came she had no doubt. Somehow, through her intense entreaties, the connection had veered off course, the cards picking up on young spirits of the dance from another time and the profound secret and mystery after which they were named as well as the dance in which they had been instructed.

She would have to move quickly to get to the farmer Gilligan for there was much to be done before the appointed hour. The people would need to be persuaded that this time all would be well and the barn must be prepared sufficiently with offerings set to bestow on their visitor.

It promised to be a fine, clear night, although bitterly cold. That at least would keep any servants of the High Sheriff close to their warm homes and unlikely to stir them even if the distinctive sound of a fiddle was carried over the countryside on the icy wind.

Although the day was still young she had swept and scrubbed the house and tidily folded snowy linen for the feather bed on which her guest would be sleeping. Every pot and pan gleamed as the weak morning rays crept through the now shiny window panes and she had raked the dirt into neat patterns in the yard so that feet of such esteem would in no way be endangered.

As she set off for Gilligan's farm with the card now pressed into the velvet pouch along with the others, she knew too that she would be responsible for guiding the dancers to their chosen destiny. They had not understood the act and language of divination that revived the lost world of soul, magical helpers and significant landscapes, although the one called Terry she was sure had not completely retreated away from nature and into himself. His eyes had been opened to all manner of possibilities and that would serve him well in the dimension to which he would return.

And so she hobbled on, her body weight assisted by her sturdy hazel stick, her sense of purpose never so keen and drawing strength from the forest that surrounded her, that army of sentient trees; the mighty oak, ferocious elms, hawthorn, willow and rowan as well as the stalwart firs. The keepers of the secrets and myths of her predecessors that would always be there long after she had turned to dust.

★

For some people life-changing moments can happen more than once. In Silas's case he knew there would never again in his lifetime be a moment so profound, so desperately, bafflingly sad and one which he was powerless to prevent. A time when the unreal finally becomes the real and the anticipation of grief becomes a kind of madness that claws at the heart and somehow finds its way into your bones.

He could still do it. He could still take her place for he believed that the message had been meant for him and him alone. And then what? There would always be a life without her. But even if she stayed he knew now that she would never allow him to love her in the way that he wanted and that would eventually create dissent in what had always been a harmonious working relationship.

"Are you okay?" Blossom was once again at his side, and for the first time since arriving at their planned location that night he became aware of the degree of frenzied activity which surrounded them.

If he didn't know better he'd have thought he'd just stepped on to the set of a movie. In fact, he wouldn't be surprised to see Steven Spielberg gliding towards them preparing for that famous one track shot, while calling for action through a large megaphone.

The place was lit with dozens of precision-beam arc lamps and enclosed within a one and a half mile radius by yards of black and yellow hazard tape. There were four portakabins, a number of police vehicles and ambulances as well as a few official looking cars parked a distance away which, as far as Silas could tell, included a black Mercedes Benz S-class and a silver Audi, both with tinted windows. That's the sinister part of the movie, he thought grimly. The scene where the guys who are supposed to be good, turn out to be the ones whom we trust the least.

The characters on the set comprised of Joe Tierney and Gerry Doyle and at least half a dozen uniformed Gardai. There was a middle-aged Priest, and Silas's curiosity was heightened by the presence of a tall albino in a dark wool coat with a fur collar. Because his imagination was now on a roll, he wondered with a kind of hallucinatory light-headedness why a supporting player from a James Bond movie would wander into a Spielberg production.

The loud whirring of a helicopter blew the trees and bushes into submission at which Blossom exploded with rage. "I told them no planes," she yelled furiously and ran in the direction of Joe Tierney, while Silas turned to see Clodagh walking towards him pulling her wheelie case. It struck him as weirder than ever that she should bring luggage. What did she have in there? Ointment for joint pain? Chocolate?

They hugged and he was once more and maybe for the last time intoxicated by the scent of her freshly washed hair and the familiar perfume of her skin. Not for her the lavish fragrances of the top designers for she always possessed her own distinctively natural aroma, a mixture of summer roses, peach and jasmine.

She was wearing a black velvet cloak that he had never seen before. It was fastened at the neck with a pewter brooch which he recognised as the design that represented the Celtic Warrior and which he assumed was specially chosen for its significance.

He slipped off his woollen gloves, stuffing them in his

pockets so that he could hold her cold hand. He felt her grasp tighten and knew that words would make no difference now to what was almost certainly inevitable. Blossom joined them as a man's voice echoed through a megaphone, not Spielberg's but Superintendent Gerry Doyle's, firm, direct and issuing instructions that each person present strained to absorb and understand.

"Ladies and gentlemen, it is precisely ten minutes to midnight. In a moment, the lights around the lake will be dimmed and I will request utter silence from all of you. When Ms. Fayard and Ms. Trevor approach we simply wait. No-one must make a sudden movement or a sudden noise during this time. Whatever you see, whatever happens after that, you must control any impulse to move towards this area or make contact with anyone until I give the order. Thank you."

The performance had begun. Clodagh gave him a look that spoke of love but for the first time he also picked up on a sense of her own empowerment and began to understand. Fingers untangled and broke away. He tried to hang on but she was leaving with Blossom and they walked swiftly and with purpose towards the predestined spot where all eyes were now focussed.

And then the wait... The final agonising trick that time was to play before the anticipated treat...if there were to be one. His eyes darted fearfully between the two women and his watch as the minutes and seconds moved towards the hour when magic was supposed to be at it's most effective. Midnight. And still they waited...Two church clocks chimed simultaneously, breaking the tense silence and which everyone except the Priest cursed for their intrusion.

Despite the freezing temperature, Silas felt his gloveless hands turn clammy and his dry mouth was crying out for water which he had forgotten to bring. Now his watch showed five past midnight and he could sense that the gathered congregation was getting restive. The small noises that humans make penetrated the desired stillness. The nervous clearing of throats, vegetation shifting beneath restless feet, excited whispers carried on the wind, and still nothing. Just the heavy blanket of intolerable suspense which pleaded to be lifted.

He wondered if the trigger factors that Blossom had explained were in fact in place. He couldn't imagine how there could be any more than were present at this moment. Surely the emotional content alone was enough to reproduce the earlier picture as well as Clodagh's readiness to accept the command, if that was how it could be described.

Then suddenly it was happening so quickly that they almost missed it. A soft, curling fog that eased itself out of the lake and drifted towards the two women, lit only by a similarly pearly moon. In an instant, Clodagh removed her long, black cloak and handed it to Blossom, who turned to make her way back up the hill and away from the manifestation.

He drew a sharp intake of breath as he saw that Clodagh was once again wearing the copy of the original costume of the High Priestess. The one that she had discarded in the fear that it was inhabiting more than just her skin. Seeming impervious to the bitter winter chill, she turned gracefully like the dancer she was and with a wave that he interpreted was meant for him and him alone, his beloved girl slipped into the silver mist and vanished from his gaze.

★

Joe Tierney stood in solemn contemplation. Gerry Doyle looked aghast. The others appeared uncertain as to what they had just witnessed. Mute and motionless, now arranged in an impressive tableau like actors in the scene from The Passion Play.

Had they really experienced something paranormal or the work of a stage illusionist? Where had the dancer gone?

Those higher up the chain of command spoke in hushed voices through lowered car windows. The barest hint of activity was tentative, draped in caution. Would

Superintendent Doyle address the group as he did before, or would they simply wait for the climax to this mysterious drama of which only a few had read the script?

Protocol demanded communication but the mist was swirling, spreading like a voluminous cloud and none of them dared to give the order to speak before it had cleared.

Blossom climbed the short distance up the hill to meet Silas halfway, where they stood gazing down towards the lake area.

She wondered if any of them had actually grasped the fact that what they had experienced was the fusion of past and present. And if that fragmentary introduction to such mystical phenomena had blown their minds then that was nothing compared to what was to come.

★

Drained and desensitised, Silas took the cloak from Blossom and buried his face into its dark softness. It still carried her scent. The velvet chrysalis after the winged insect had flown.

Then, alerted by a collective gasp that fluttered around the site and sensing that Blossom was tugging at his arm, he raised his head.

He hardly recognised them, for their body shapes seemed to have changed. As they stumbled out of the fog, clinging to one another, tearful and bewildered, he immediately noticed that some of the thinner ones were carrying more weight, while the ones that had built up muscle through years of training were far slighter. On every one the torn and soiled clothes they were wearing hung like rags on a scarecrow.

The boys appeared dazed and confused and had grown beards and hair that touched their shoulders. The girls were uncombed, with complexions duller than before, and he felt an overwhelming longing to run towards them, envelope them in his arms and welcome them home with all the love and relief that their safe return deserved.

They were being instructed to line up behind the taped barricade by four figures clad from head to foot in nuclear protective clothing. It was a scene that Silas and Blossom found dauntingly familiar to those they had enjoyed over the years accompanied by cartons of popcorn. These menacing figures then proceeded to select each nervous dancer individually in order to pass radioactive detectors across every area of their bodies as well as their hand luggage before guiding them towards the waiting ambulances.

Both he and Blossom were desperate for answers to the torrent of questions that were now waging war on their minds. Had Blossom's theory about a Dance Master been correct? Who had been communicating to them through the Tarot? Had they encountered Clodagh on the way out of the past? So many answers which maybe they would never get to hear, for it was obvious that after being thoroughly checked over for any contamination, his troupe would be whisked away for de-briefing before finally returning to the arms of their loving families.

The lake had returned to its former serenity leaving not even a whisper of fog and the set was being struck. Joe Tierney and Gerry Doyle had released the uniformed Gardai who made their way to their respective cars. Some of the lamps were dismantled but there was just enough light for the activity which was continuing near the portakabins and ambulances, and the cars which Silas assumed belonged to government officials waited silently for their cue to participate in the extravaganza.

He noticed that the albino with the fur-collared coat had been collected and accompanied away by a paramedic. Only the Priest remained, and on seeing Silas turn around, hurried towards them.

"Mysterious ways…" he said, breathlessly, tugging at his cassock in order to keep his balance on the grassy incline. "How are you, my son?"

The enormous lump that had settled in his throat prevented him from speaking and the Priest nodded towards

Blossom who saved him from the embarrassment of a non-reply.

"Silas and Clodagh were very close." She told him. "He's not sure if he'll ever get to see her again."

"I understand." It was an obvious statement in the circumstances, but then he surprised them by saying. "I came to know her quite well. During the last few months."

So, he was from the church in Ennis that she used to visit. Silas held her cloak even closer, like a child with a security blanket that he would never allow out of his sight.

"I was asked to come here by Superintendent Doyle," the Priest continued. "He thought I might be of some assistance."

He glanced towards the area where the dancers were being held. "If I can be of no help to you, Silas, then I will see if there's anything I can do for them."

Silas loosened his grip on Clodagh's cloak and in a voice that quivered with the despair he was now feeling, startled Blossom by blurting out.

"It seems I am experiencing the one sin that cannot be forgiven, Father. So pray for me."

★

The Huffington Post. December 2015.
"Mystery of Arcanum dancers solved?"
Article by Victoria Kline

It is now nearly two weeks since the Irish dance troupe Arcanum was discovered in County Clare in the Republic of Ireland having escaped from a remote location where they had been held captive by person or persons unknown after one of the greatest search operations in history.

The Co. Clare Garda and officials from the CIB have been unusually coy about releasing information regarding the circumstances in which the twenty-five young people were abducted and it is believed that their captors absconded with the tour bus and as yet have not been caught and apprehended.

Some of the dancers who have spoken to the media have described the bus as having broken down just off the M18 while on diversion to Ennis following an earlier accident in the early hours of Tuesday 15th September.

They have described being led to a farmer's outbuildings by an elderly woman where they were informed they could not be released as they would be arrested. The farmer, who told them his name was Mick, forced them to sleep in a barn where they were fed simple food and guarded over by a fierce black dog.

They have spoken of arriving at their destination in a dense fog and released at night in similar weather conditions, making it almost impossible to pinpoint exactly where they were being held. There appeared to be no electricity connected to the farm and they were unable to obtain signals on their cells and tablets.

The driver of the tour bus, Dubliner Dennis Ahearne, managed to escape his captors and, as this publication reported, has been suffering from a severe psychiatric disorder since his discovery at Lough Rosroe, Co. Clare in late October.

The denouement of this mystery, far from having put an end to speculation, has only served to fuel the hundreds of thousands of conspiracy theories that are flooding the internet and re-ignited a massive interest in the area as the search for the farmhouse and its owner continues.

To add to the labyrinth of conjecture two further incidents may stimulate further examination.

While American lead dancer and choreographer Silas Murphy, thirty two, has given a statement to the press confirming his relief and delight at the dancers' safe return, Irish born Clodagh Trevor, twenty-four, the group's willowy leading female dancer has been unavailable for comment, stunning fans by her failure to post anything about the event on either her Facebook or Twitter pages. Her family who live in Donnybrook, Co. Dublin have maintained a dignified silence regarding her whereabouts.

There is also the case of Terence Riley, the thirty year old stage manager who was kidnapped alongside the dancers *and who has consistently refused to speak to anyone about the abduction. As this writer learned a few days ago, Mr. Riley has recently entered a Cistercian Abbey in County Waterford.*

★

If it had been his choice, then the last place in the world Joe Tierney would have wanted to be that night was at his daughter's Christmas feis. Forced to sit through two and a half solid hours of Irish competitive dancing for girls between the ages of fourteen and sixteen, he was unable to keep his thoughts from returning to the events of the last few weeks. Then, when Sacha was announced as winner in the solo reel category, he pulled himself back from his wanderings and rose along with the other parents to applaud and cheer before pushing past his astonished wife and son out of the drill hall and into the Dublin street.

Leaning against a wall that separated the hall from a church filled with carol singers, he welcomed the sting of fresh snow on his face and tried to free his mind from what had happened that night by the lake. What *had* happened?

There had been no time for contemplation. Caught in a vortex of high-powered and top security meetings and conference calls with those who normally he would never have encountered, he now had become two people and the strain was marked by his recent weight loss, short concentration span and sleeplessness.

Sure, he had kept secrets before. Had to tell white lies. It went with the territory and he had accepted and balanced these numerous incidents with never a guilty thought or the temptation to disclose facts that might throw a case into jeopardy or compromise anyone's privacy or trust in the Garda in which he had loyally served for thirty years.

Until now. And because this was so other, so totally off the Richter scale, he had felt the overwhelming need to share what he had witnessed with the people closest to him and his inability to do this through duty was pulling him in such polar directions that only complete withdrawal seemed the obvious course of action.

Therefore, Joe Tierney found himself in a worrying and uncomfortable place not helped by the fact that Sacha was obsessed with Arcanum. She had spoken of little else during their disappearance and even more since their return. The small amount of time he had spent with her so far during this school holiday season had resulted in a bombardment of endless questions for news of their kidnappers and even more for news of Clodagh Trevor whom she had idolised.

And his wife who knew him so well of course realised he was hiding something big. Something of national importance. She could see it in his eyes and sensed it in his change of demeanour but she knew better than to probe, understanding that the price he would have to pay for disclosing classified information would mean the end of his career.

Then there was the little matter of the gold coins which had been found in the possession of the stage manager. Twelve of them, dating from the early seventeenth century. They of course had now been whisked away by forensics and God knows where from there but the kids had started to enquire when they might have them back as they wanted to cash them in and share the profits between them.

And so they should. They said they were a gift and so by rights they owned them, but he was sure they would never be returned. The stage manager had not put up a fight when asked to hand them over and Joe was pretty certain that he was the only member of the group who really knew the truth about their capture.

He could hear Irish music starting up again in counterpoint with the carols and realised that Sacha must have accepted her trophy and was now doing her lap of honour. As he turned to go back in, he came face to face with Peggy O'Neill and knew there was no escape from a confrontation.

"Hello Superintendent." She said closing the door

behind her and preventing his entering. "I saw you come out and thought I'd chance having a quiet word."

"Miss O'Neill." He nodded. "I have to go back. Sacha…"

The dance mistress cut across him briskly. "Yes, she won. Deservedly so."

"Thank you." He said haplessly. "You've been a marvellous teacher to her."

The resemblance to Clodagh was quite uncanny. Red hair tinged with grey was piled into an untidy but oddly sexy knot framing a face with the same fine cheekbones and remarkable olive green eyes that were now searching his for answers.

"I know you know where my niece is. I just want you to give our family the assurance that she is safe."

How could he do that? He had absolutely no idea.

"I'm afraid I don't know where Clodagh is, Miss O'Neill. But I'm sure that when she is ready to return, she will let you know."

How cold. How matter-of-fact shitty cold. He couldn't have hated himself more than he did at that moment, standing on an icy pavement on a bleak December night with this delightful woman who simply wanted the truth. If it had been Sacha instead of Clodagh who had disappeared, he would not have just asked politely after her whereabouts, but would probably have threatened violence.

Peggy O'Neill tugged her red cashmere scarf a little tighter round her neck and took a step closer towards him.

"I understand that your hands are tied, Superintendent. But just answer me one thing, please? Did Clodagh go wherever she is of her own free will?

He was grateful for small mercies for this time he didn't have to lie.

"She did."

The woman gave him a long, sad stare then turned towards the door.

"Thank you, Superintendent. Now, shall we go and congratulate Sacha?"

Silas moved robotically among the crowds of Christmas shoppers, street performers and musicians, pausing to inhale the tempting aroma of sizzling chestnuts then weaving his unchartered way between lines of trees twinkling with fairy lights and hung with tiny gift boxes tantalising in their shiny red and green wrapping.

It was still hard for him to believe that he was spending Christmas at home instead of on the road with Arcanum. It was a state that six months ago he would never have predicted and even stranger was that this time he was not just visiting but had made the relatively easy decision to return for good, moving back in with his parents and, with Blossom's help, bringing all of his possessions over from Dublin.

Boston did Christmas well and it wasn't just because it resembled the Irving Berlin picture of how it should be. As he grabbed a hot chocolate from one of the stalls and made a half-hearted attempt at window shopping, he continued through the cobbled triangle of the market place to the strains of Johnny Mathis, negotiated a giant reindeer and passed a dim grotto where children were gathered around the rotund figure of a Coca Cola Santa.

The glue that had been holding him together during the ordeal had lost much of its strength, causing a wave of fatigue which had now become a regular and unwelcome visitor. For someone who had always prided himself on his fitness Silas sank onto a bench, reminded once again that it was all gone. Every trace of those years of hard slog had disappeared along with the drifting Irish mist and the woman he could not forget.

His dancers had scattered and showed no appetite at the moment to return to work. Nor had he the desire nor energy to consider forming a new troupe or choreographing another set routine as spectacular as that which had been fated to enjoy so short an existence. But life had taught him never to say never and it was always possible that one day he might find the heart to resurrect it although the wounds were still too open and too fresh to attempt such an emotional undertaking in the foreseeable future.

Now he had to try and get his life into some sort of shape and to re-charge his desperately depleted batteries. He licked the last of the whipped cream from the top of his drink and pondered on the offers that had flooded in from publishers asking him to pen an account of the whole affair accompanied by a hefty advance.

Of course that was impossible but he had flirted with the idea of writing a true account and suggesting they market it as a work of fiction. A novel. A story of courage, sacrifice and hope. That way he could possibly get around the secrecy documents he had signed and produce a pretty good story.

But he knew they wouldn't want that. What they wanted was a true account where he would have to lie. The irony of it didn't escape him and he smiled to himself, receiving an intrigued stare from a little girl in a matching tartan hat and coat being pulled along by her mother and who continued to stare until she disappeared into one of the many busy stores.

Silas realised there and then that in the whole of his adult life he had never felt so lonely. He stood up and aimed his cup expertly into the trash can, remembering how he and Clodagh used to advocate positive thinking whenever things got rough. Now it seemed that positive thinking had become wishful thinking, manifesting in the shame of not having taken her place, praying for her safe return and trying never to allow his mind to embrace the possibility of the worse terrors that might have claimed her.

He wandered on, nudged by men, women and children only intent on seasonal pursuits and struggled to concentrate his thoughts on gifts for Blossom and for his family. As he rounded a corner he happened upon a shop that he had passed many times over the years but had never gone into. The Irish Shop, nestling between a book store and a

Starbucks was designed as *Olde Worlde* with Dickensian style windows of bubbly plate-glass framed with highly polished wood and, as he peered inside, Silas saw a cosy interior lit by brass oil lamps.

It looked so inviting that he found himself opening the door and stepping in, an old fashioned bell jingling his arrival, but feeling that it was probably a silly thing to do as he had just returned from the country itself and could have purchased anything this shop had to offer when he was living there.

He glanced around at the collection of up-market Aran sweaters delicately woven from silk as well as the traditional fisherman's jumpers, woollen hats with matching scarves and tweed caps and coats. There were neatly folded napkins of the finest Irish linen and the usual collection of souvenirs; mugs painted with leprechauns and shamrocks, Guinness place mats and snow globes containing miniature Irish dancers.

Idly he picked up one of the globes and shook it, releasing a snow storm that swirled around the glass and as he turned the key it tinkled out a tune that he recognised but couldn't name.

Immediately the figure of the dancer began to move inside the globe and the snow slowly settled. Peering closer, Silas examined the tiny form in its short green dress, then released a sharp gasp of shock at the doll's features for they seemed to distinctly resemble Clodagh's.

He glanced wildly around but there was no-one else in the shop, not even a salesperson, and he closed his eyes for a second then opened them, once again cursing what this whole affair had done to him. There had been so many tricks played on his mind which turned out not to be tricks at all, that it was becoming impossible to tell the difference between what was his imagination and what was not. Of course it was just a plastic figure and it could have been fashioned on any Irish dancer. Slim with red hair and now as he examined it closer, a pale glyptic face forced into a set smile.

What was wrong with him? And why was he so pathetically

searching for signs, anything that would signal a message from her letting him know she was okay? His shrink would have said it was all part of the mourning process, but as his shrink had been given the heave-ho because he thought that he was fantasising, Silas was unable to bring a molecule of logic to his thought processes.

He wanted to buy it although his brain was screaming to his heart that it wasn't a sign or a message, just a dancing doll in a globe, not even made in Ireland or here in America, but in China.

He turned with a start as someone emerged from the back of the shop. A tall young man with wavy dark hair and wearing a green sweater which sported the knitted figure of a large snowman in a top hat.

"Can I help?"

Silas handed the globe over and rummaged into his leather shoulder bag. "How much?"

"One hundred and twenty-five," the sales assistant told him and as he produced some wrapping paper from beneath the counter, he lowered his voice and leaned forward.

"Don't I know you from somewhere?"

"I don't think so." Silas was now eager to make his purchase and get on his way. The last thing he needed was casual conversation.

"Sure I do." The man persisted. "You're that dancer, Silas Murphy. Hell, we were all pleased as punch that they were found."

Silas activated his credit card and accepted his wrapped gift. "Thank you."

But the young man hadn't finished with his customer yet.

"Mr. Murphy, can I ask, do you believe in coincidences?"

It was a question that came so out of the blue that once again it pulled Silas up short and caused him to pause by the door. Remembering how Blossom had dismissed the term as intellectual laziness, he was prompted to answer. "As a matter of fact, no. Why?"

The young man's face had now become flushed and his eyes gleamed with excitement as he stepped from behind the counter, beckoning Silas to follow him through to the back of the shop.

"Because I was offered something last week which I think might be of interest to you. Come…"

Hesitating, Silas then allowed his curiosity to get the better of him and slowly followed where he was being led. It struck him as a familiar cliché, that ultimate item which shops of this kind dealing in souvenirs and historic content always seemed to find for the perfect customer. Or the perfect gullible idiot.

It was a storeroom piled high with cardboard boxes and the contrast to the dimly lit shop was marked by the strong strip lighting above their heads, turning the shadow of their faces to the pallor of death masks.

The salesman lifted a long item wrapped in tissue paper from behind a filing cabinet and began to peel the paper away as Silas looked on intrigued. He watched as the item emerged and saw that it appeared to be a gentleman's cane, but far sturdier than most he had seen. It was highly polished with a silver handle and he could feel just by looking at it that it was very old indeed.

"A woman who lives here in Boston brought it in last week," the young man told him. "She said it had been handed down through generations of her family who were Irish and who came over to America in the early nineteenth century. I took a look at it and asked her why she hadn't taken it to an auction house or a museum as it was obviously of some historical value."

Silas was still unsure as to why he should be singled out for this information, but there was something that was keeping his eyes fastened on the object the salesman was holding. An indefinable but fascinating something.

"She told me that she chose to bring it here because she was sure that someone who came to this shop would want to buy it and treasure it. It was rumoured to have been an old Dance Master's staff which was used when these guys were going around Ireland teaching folks who wanted to learn to dance. She said she had taken it to an antiques expert who told her that it was difficult to tell what kind of wood it was made of as it had been lacquered over so many times, but he thought that it might not have been made in Ireland because it was too sophisticated. He guessed it was possibly from Europe. Maybe as early as the 17th century."

Silas began to feel the familiar tingle of excitement coupled with an assault on his nerve-ends that caused his skin to turn hot and then prickly cold. He wished that Blossom was here and could bring her usual sense of practicality to that which was strange and bewildering to him.

"Did she say what part of Ireland they were from? Her family?" He heard himself asking as though through a long, echoey tunnel.

"She did as a matter of fact." The salesman replied. "County Clare. Which of course you know."

He wanted to laugh but knowing it would come out sounding like a hyena on speed, suppressed it.

The young man moved towards him, holding out the cane with reverent respect.

"When you came in today I knew you were the one that she meant it for. Coincidence or not, it's for you."

Something stopped him from accepting it straight away, for outside influences were moving a little too swiftly for his liking.

"What do you want for it?"

"I gave her five thousand dollars. In cash. I don't want to make a profit, just to see it in the hands it belongs."

He would have a problem raising that kind of money in his current position. Maybe he would write that book after all.

That was when Silas reached out for the cane and felt her touch on it immediately. The poignant sensation was as sweet as warm maple syrup drizzled over ice cream and he could not help but utter a long sigh which turned into her name.

"Clodagh…"

Nature could erase traces of the past but this inanimate object had proved that it could carry the past with it in a way that was both mystical and material. He was sure that this cane bore a history that whispered of many joys and sorrows long before Clodagh had held it in her hands.

This then was what he had been longing for. Something that told him she was okay and had maybe thought enough of him to find a way to send a message down through the decades to comfort him in his grief and solitude. Being in love with a ghost would have haunted him forever and perhaps now he could move forward with his life and a future that promised the hope and fulfilment that he had always known.

CO. CLARE.
1735

The beginning of her journey of discovery far exceeded anything she had imagined, for as the silvery fog drew her in, it became impossible to see beyond its density. It was as if she was levitating on a tread-mill of air pulled by an invisible magnet and yet not seeming to cover any distance.

A slight ringing in her ears caused her to shake her head, but the sensation was not unpleasant. She dug deep into her imagination and visualised tinkling silver bells until a swift whooshing sound suddenly took their place and caused her heart to accelerate. A salmon leaping from a stream perhaps? Or the rushing whistle of birds' wings?

How long the osmosis had taken was impossible to guess. When every sound had faded, borne away on the mist, she knew instinctively that she was in the same place she had left, but in another time.

After travelling through so much light, darkness struck like an inky canopy and as her feet found solid ground, she gasped in anticipation and awe. She had prepared herself for her exile and now the moment had arrived with all its mystery and uncertainty.

At first her brain struggled to digest the shapes she thought she recognised. The familiar curve of the mountains stamped against a sky filled with the most magnificent stars. The same moon, full and golden. Forests of trees far denser than those left behind, and…was that large, dark object that loomed silently to her left…could that really be the coach?

And then the unfamiliar. A flash from a lantern and a hand touching her arm causing her to almost faint from shock.

Turning, Clodagh came face to face with the old woman and knew immediately that she was the one who had been communicating with them through the Tarot.

"Hello." Clodagh greeted her quietly, thinking that perhaps there would be uncertainty on both sides.

The old woman nodded but didn't speak. She smiled widely and Clodagh was saddened to see what few teeth she had remaining were black and rotting. She was dressed in what appeared to be several layers of full skirts and a grey woollen shawl was draped around her shoulders.

But there was something she was carrying in a sack that seemed to excite her and she placed the lantern on a low stone wall, untying the string that held the sack together and digging her hand down into its rough depths with a chortle that reminded Clodagh of such solitary crones she had only read about in fairy tales.

Barely visible in the low light, Clodagh gazed with wonder on what the woman had produced from the sack and was now pushing towards her, insisting with grunts and gestures that she should accept and wear the garment.

It was a beautiful coat. Purple and gold, braided with ribbons of the most dazzling, colours Clodagh had ever seen embroidered into one costume. If this had belonged to an old Dance Master, then how could it be that it was still so bright? She slipped her arms into it and immediately became aware of her seven centres of energy awakening to embrace the colours and resonating with their vibrancies against her body. Cerise and acquamarine, sherbert and emerald shimmered in the lantern's glow.

For Clodagh, this presented the alchemy of transformation into the person she was now to become. The coat was her own personal armour against whatever perils lay ahead, and together with the Priestess costume and her gold cross it was all the protection she needed.

A scarlet hat with a purple feather was then proffered and Clodagh accepted it gracefully, fixing it over her long hair and completing the outfit to the satisfaction of the old woman who cackled with delight before looking down at her shoes with a gasp.

Clodagh was wearing her soft dance pumps with the long white laces that criss-crossed over the top of her feet and tied around her ankles and it was clear that no foot-wear as delicately fashioned existed at this time, particularly in such rural surroundings.

"Ahhh…" was all the woman managed to emit and nodded vigorously once again as they suddenly became aware of the sound of men's voices, the whinnying of a horse and a blaze of light panning across the fields in the distance.

A vision was advancing towards them and she could only liken it to an historical ceremonial procession. Lighted torches were held by what appeared to be at least forty men of various ages, half of whom walked either side of a cart pulled by a large, grey horse. If this was her welcoming committee then it was certainly both impressive and dramatic.

The torches burned and flared, sending smoke and sparks billowing into the night air as their carriers approached and Clodagh could just make out the figure of a tall man who was driving the cart. She stood nervously fidgeting with the ribbons on her coat as they drew closer and when he pulled up next to them, watched with fascination as the man sprang out, clearly expecting a visitor, but not her.

The group shuffled forward then froze, the older ones' leathery faces lined with the maps of their lives, their eyes piercing and expectant. They bore the weary signs of those who had been waiting for a miracle and Clodagh bit her lip, the acrid taste of smoke on her tongue, wondering if she was meant to be that miracle and praying that she could live up to it's expectations if that was so.

The driver of the cart who had kind brown eyes but was not smiling, addressed his opening words to the old woman.

"Cad é seo?" ("What's this?")

The old woman frowned, then gestured towards Clodagh, her hand sweeping down the front of the coat as if to demonstrate the treasure she had uncovered, but the man and his companions remained agitated.

"Bean, nach bhfuil?" ("A woman?")

Clodagh swallowed her fear and decided to speak up, hoping that the man would understand English.

"Hello, my name is Clodagh. I'm your new Dance Master."

"Ye can't be a Dance Master. You're a woman!" He spat in a thick brogue and the others surrounding him nodded in agreement, muttering to one another and gazing at Clodagh with a mixture of disappointment and frustration at discovering her gender, while the torches they each were holding seemed to flicker with a less celebratory flame.

She stood her ground, knowing that this delicate negotiation had to be approached with caution and determination. If Blossom was correct and this community really did believe they were under the influence of some curse, then she had to be the one to convince them that she could lift it.

"I've come a long way, sir, in order to help your people learn and enjoy the dance and I'm not giving up just because you want a man instead of a woman. May I ask what happened to your last Dance Master?"

The owner of the cart suddenly appeared uneasy and gave her a long stare. His eyes then scanned the group and he spoke to them in Irish, before turning back to Clodagh.

"Aye, then. Jump up."

As he held out his hand to assist her climb into the rough, wooden vehicle, she breathed a relieved sigh knowing that a small battle won did not mean a victorious war, for her work had not yet begun. The old woman clambered in beside her, rearranging her long skirts as the horse was instructed to trot towards some unknown destination.

The lullaby of night caressed them as the rhythm of the hooves and the moving lights led the way along a well-travelled path and one which Clodagh was sure her friends must have taken. She wondered how they were and if they'd returned safely but these were all questions that would have to wait. The torch bearers were scrutinising her so intently that it seemed they were branding her a traitor. And yet somehow she didn't feel threatened. Just chastised and scorned. She could handle that until she proved them wrong. She fingered the small golden cross only to be forced out of a prayer by the clamour of voices, the cries of infants and a fiddler striking up a jig.

Rising from the discomfort of the rickety seat and trying to maintain her balance, her eyes were momentarily blinded by a large square of brightness which at first glance resembled a giant movie screen. As the cart slowed down, she realised that she was gazing into an open barn where iron lanterns hung from the rafters and scattered in dark corners spinning a mirage of light towards them. She peered closer and saw that the straw had been swept away from the stone ground and where the surface had obviously become uneven, two large wooden doors had been removed from their hinges and laid down to cover and flatten the area.

Clodagh knew at once that this was the place which had been prepared for dancing and where she was destined to begin her long awaited task. As the grey horse brought them to a jerky halt, stamping and shaking its mane, she took the hand of the driver and alighted to even more scrutiny. This time from her own sisterhood.

The assorted group of women stared and shook their heads and while some were fascinated, others were plainly unhappy to learn that their new tutor was a woman. Some were so full of curiosity that they came close enough to touch her and then, as if not sure that she was human, sprang back warily, scattering like nervous hens sensing the presence of a fox in their midst.

Clodagh understood. Even through the shared identity of their species, she would seem so very different to them. It wasn't just her scent, but the texture of her hair and skin, the whiteness of her teeth and her manner of movement.

It would be hard to guess their ages, but even at such a late hour some were carrying babies or toddlers and she would have put them all above twenty years. Despite their obvious slender means it was clear they had made a real effort for many were wearing similar black skirts embroidered with green and white Celtic designs of animals and flowers and she noticed that while their faces were free of make-up, they kept pinching their cheeks and lips in order to give themselves colour.

She looked around for the young people. The teenagers. Although that word had yet to be invented. No-one present seemed to be between the ages of twelve and twenty and she was puzzled, believing that they would have been the age group that were the most keen to learn how to express themselves through the dance.

As the men-folk continued further up the hill to toss the now smouldering torches on to a crackling bonfire, she realised that the tall man who had been driving the cart must be the farmer who lived here as he appeared to be taking charge and trying to coax the women and children inside the barn.

"What is your name?" She asked him, venturing to touch his arm.

"Mick," he told her. "Mick Gilligan and ye've got your work cut out."

"I know that, Mick. I will do my best." Before letting him go, she had to ask. "Did you see my friends?"

He knew at once what she meant and his answer lifted her spirits more than she could have believed possible.

"Aye. Thee've gone."

Choked with relief, she felt a sudden tug on her coat and looking down saw a little girl with rosy cheeks and hair the colour of mustard seed. In her hand she was clutching a bunch of deep pink heather which she thrust towards Clodagh, prompted by her pretty mother who smiled shyly while hovering nearby.

"How lovely. Thank you so much." Clodagh told the child, and then glanced towards the mother, unsure as to whether she understood but hoping she would realise how appreciated the gesture was.

With a growing sense of dismay she watched as Mick Gilligan struggled to persuade the reluctant men and women into his barn, for she knew that the Penal laws were still in force and that he would be anxious to close his doors so as not to be heard by those who might see fit to condemn and punish this innocent tradition.

It became obvious that soon she would have to exercise some control as any male in her place would, and as she searched her mind for the way to begin, the old woman appeared at her side folding a slim cane with a curved silver handle into her hands with a sense of urgency. Unsure what to do with this latest offering, Clodagh then remembered she had read that the Dance Masters often used staffs to assist in their teaching, although this was no ordinary wooden staff but a handsome, highly polished prop that might well serve in her introduction to the lesson. At the very least it could be used to attract their attention.

Gathering her courage, she tried to ignore those still lingering and whispering by the entrance and with a sudden swift movement brought the cane down hard on one of the wooden doors that had been laid for dancing.

The voices tapered off and something close to a silence dropped onto a space where it now felt as though the life of the world had been suspended.

With more force than she realised she was capable of and

praying that the cane wouldn't snap, Clodagh once again beat it hard against the wood under her feet. Now a few of the group moved closer, eyes wide, curiosity ignited as they formed a horseshoe arc and Mick Gilligan pulled the heavy barn doors shut after the last trickle of men slipped inside.

She had no idea how to cue the music as the poor fiddler was blind and was also sleeping, so in the firmest voice she could manage called out loudly for a jig. In an instant he shot up like a jack-in-the-box toy cranked from his slumber and Clodagh forced herself to recall a military style routine she had performed at the World Championship in Philadelphia in 2009. This cane was longer than a baton, but she was sure she could manage to twirl it if the sleeves of her coat allowed her movement.

As the traditional lilt cut through an atmosphere of ardent expectation, she moved spontaneously into a single jig, a dance that she had performed numerous versions of over the years and one which she was sure they would find engaging if accompanied by arm movements. Gripping the cane firmly with both hands for the first eight bars of the music, Clodagh then began to swing it deftly between her right and left shoulders, bringing it forward and back then swinging it again, while keeping in time with her intricate footwork.

It was a dizzying routine based on balance and she lost herself in the moment as the speed rose and fell for it was the prologue to the lesson she was sure would follow.

As she slowed to a halt and caught the cane with one hand in a dramatic flourish, she could not fail to be aware of the number of eyes boring into her, the souls who were judging her, open-mouthed and most disconcertingly of all – quiet.

And so she waited. Waited for the nourishment that every artiste craves but that can be served either hot or cold. But this was so very different. This time she needed more than ever to be appreciated and accepted and this was no competition or first night. Their approval would ratify her very existence in a place that would turn her from a stranger into someone they could learn to love and respect and more importantly who would try to provide that welcome light they had been waiting for.

The atmosphere of numbed hypnosis was finally broken by the beautiful child who had given her the heather and who squealed and clapped her tiny hands, but no-one else joined in and Clodagh tried to think beyond the flood of anxiety that was threatening to drown her.

What would Silas do now? Auntie Peggy? She was pretty sure they would have said 'first steps first'. Had she gone in too strong when the most basic of routines would have been where to start? She had tried to entertain them with something skilful but instead of capturing their interest she had merely overwhelmed them. Now, she had to pull the proverbial rabbit out of her plumed hat.

Glancing down at their feet she noticed that all the men were wearing their hard reel shoes and the women who weren't barefoot were wearing their black lace up ghillies. The shoes looked clumsy and were obviously nailed roughly in the toes and the heels but this was what they had all come to dance in. Stepping off the wooden door Clodagh ran to her wheelie case and zipped it open, stemming curiosity once more as she pulled out her hard shoes and changed quickly.

Back on the wooden surface she cued the fiddler for another tune. This time she kept her arms stiffly at her sides and began to click and tap with the fibreglass heels and toes, working up a strong percussive rhythm as she performed a hard treble jig, but at a slower pace than before thereby fitting more steps into its 6/8 tempo.

"Treble down," she heard herself saying loudly, invoking the spirit of auntie Peggy's teaching voice echoing through many a classroom. "Let's go!"

With each beat and click from the old style step-dancing she was now performing, she saw the assembled crowd begin to instinctively feel the music. Even the older ones, tentative at first, still slow to trust, moved their toes and heels separately into the melody then gradually followed the speed she was setting before working up to a faster pace.

"Come," she said, releasing her arms from their rigidity to motion them closer. "Come, please?"

The younger men were the first to cast off their inhibitions and prejudices and to Clodagh's immense relief and delight she then heard the sound of their feet begin to pound upon the hard surface of the barn floor.

Some of them now had joined her on the two wooden doors and were dancing alongside her. They kept their bodies straight but their ankles were supple and their footwork surprisingly precise. As the fiddler increased the tempo they each performed their own version of the jig and when the women joined in, their long hair flying, skirts spinning, Clodagh whispered a silent prayer of gratitude, half Christian, half Pagan, to God and the High Priestess.

Now the thunder of their steps was finally ebbing away and the fiddler lowered his bow while she exhaled the longest breath of her life then clapped her hands as she walked around them showing her approval. Suddenly she knew her role was not simply to teach them. Someone brilliant had already seen to that. They had to be encouraged and the change in their demeanours from beaten and world weary to joyful and energised was enough to convince her that her unpredictable journey had not been in vain.

Awash in sweat but eager to carry on, the men jostled and boxed one another playfully like schoolboys, the older ones' swarthy faces suddenly transformed with the glow of youth. The women, high from a rush of pure adrenalin noticed that Clodagh had unbuttoned her coat, and appearing to no longer consider her a threat, moved to admire her Priestess costume as well as daring to touch her gold cross in fascination and wonder.

A plump woman with a florid complexion and long grey hair whom Clodagh assumed to be the farmer Gilligan's wife, was passing chipped earthenware cups around for sharing, filled from a large copper bowl held by a lad who was probably their son. As the hot whisky drink laced with honey and cranberries was spooned into her cup, she took a cautious sip and felt its warmth travel down to her stomach then spread upwards again until it reached her head in a tingling glow, adding to the pure physical pleasure she had just been experiencing.

She glanced towards the barn doors where the farmer and the old woman were huddled together in what appeared to be an intense and conspiratorial exchange. They stared at her then quickly looked away and she wondered whether it was some sort of signal to join them before the dancing resumed.

But before she could make that decision, Mick Gilligan lifted the two heavy wooden bars that unlocked the wide doors and walked outside. Startled and then beginning to worry, she passed her cup to one of the women and moved forward. The dancing had only just begun so why was the farmer opening the doors now?

As the voices of those around her hummed like a thousand nesting bees and the fiddler changed his tune to a country air, Clodagh found herself, as she had done so many times over the last few months, standing on the edge of her imagination, gazing into the unknown.

The nightscape she had left behind when entering the barn had changed. A few more lanterns had been hung on the skeletal limbs of trees that surrounded the farmhouse throwing a magical glow against a sky which was now starless and breathing out a whirling cloud of snow flakes that danced in the wind before silently touching the ground and melted before her eyes.

Mesmerised by such a picturesque sight, Clodagh moved slowly towards the barn doors where the old woman sat grinning. What was going on? Was this yet another test and how many more hoops would she have to skip through before passing it?

Then out of the shadows she saw Mick striding back towards the barn, but he was not alone. Trailing behind him were others. Human forms in bright clothes of various lengths and designs. It was then with an aching stab of half-forgotten memories and with tears streaming freely down her face, that she recognised the costumes which they had obviously found. Every kind of emotion she had ever known and some she had never experienced until now surfaced and spilled over into a fountain of joy and loss.

The young people had arrived. As she wiped away her tears she looked into their wishful faces and a new strength flooded through her body. However thin from lack of nutrition, however burdened from working from an early age, their smiling eyes seemed to be only embracing the moment which was now, and they could hardly wait to free their spirits with the magic of movement and music.

Blossom and the old woman would have said this was indeed Magic. And the costumes were playing their part not just for the boys and girls who were wearing them but for every man, woman and child who were gathering to appreciate and touch them. These wonderful creations taken from the Major and Minor suits of the Tarot were, through their ancient symbolism of light and shadow as well as their more recent association with the Celtic Cross, making a profound comment on Ireland's cultural and religious history at this time.

Each costumed figure was greeted with a hug from Clodagh for it was as though she had known them forever. The Magician and the Page of Cups linked arms as they made their way into the barn followed by the Empress and the Hermit, characters that she had danced alongside but whose occupants were now those who would never experience the feverish thrill of performing in a proper theatre or responding to rapturous applause from a thousand faces.

Once inside, Mick Gilligan pulled the giant bars across the doors and while the excitement provided by the costumes was still in full swing, Clodagh gave herself a moment to reflect before moving on to the next phase of their tutelage where she would persuade them that they could slowly introduce more freedom of arm movement into some of the dances while at the same time never surrendering the strong traditional individualism of their heritage.

How tenuous a concept happiness was. How it fed the souls of not just those who were experiencing it but for a visitor from another time as she had become.

But it was a lonely feeling knowing what lay ahead for their country. Those whose fate was linked with hers were suffering hard times but they would never experience the grim horror that their descendants would be destined to suffer in the cholera epidemic of 1832 or the mass starvation due to the now infamous Great Famine.

She shuddered. A ghost passing over her grave perhaps? This was for the future. Or was it the past? Suddenly Clodagh felt the two dissolve and fracture in the blink of an eye.

She started to walk towards the group aware that during the lifetime of some of those present the chains of repression would soon be loosened and the barn doors would be thrown open to allow the light and the music to flood freely into every corner of the county without fear.

Consoled by this foreknowledge, she buttoned up her coat, reached for the silver-topped cane and stepped onto the wooden platform confident that the energy that existed within this space right now would continue to haunt and linger down through the ages. As it already had.

★

"Job done!" Erin Shaw rose from her chair in the empty theatre office and snapped her lap top shut then replaced the credit card in her pink Chanel clutch.

She gathered the reams of paper from the printer and flicked through them with an expression of feline satisfaction which sat well on her perfectly painted face.

This was where it started. The illustrated copies of the costumes sent from the costumier in New York had now been bought and paid for and on Monday morning she would instruct her dressmaker in Dublin to make a start on re-creating the designs for her troupe of dancers. For Lighthouse.

Erin could not help but feel excited. She now had the scenery and the props and would soon finish choreographing the Tarot finale in which she would make sure that the music and the steps were ever so slightly different to that which Silas Murphy had originated.

Of course the world had yet to hear of Lighthouse but the world already knew of Arcanum and the routine would be announced as a tribute to a company whose name had been on most people's lips for the past four months of this year. A company who had experienced their fair share of drama and adventure and who now had conveniently disbanded.

She hadn't seen Silas to say goodbye and where Clodagh had gone was yet another mystery. But Erin already had her Australian and New Zealand tours in place for next year and had approached Las Vegas and a few other U.S. venues where Arcanum had been poised to perform during the following year as well as marking in The O2 in Dublin and in London for future engagements if the show lived up to expectations.

She knew that Silas had not signed any contracts with these venues so it all looked pretty rosy and she surmised that it was even possible that a few of the original dancers might feel inclined to join her troupe at some later stage.

All in all, Erin was delighted with her hard work and seemingly good fortune and would now go back to her home in Newmarket-on-Fergus, open a good bottle of wine and toast her future and that of the set dance which would make her name on the circuit as well as turning her euros into dollars.

Folding the designs into her briefcase with such infinite care they might have been the Dead Sea Scrolls, she prepared to leave the theatre, throwing on her faux fur coat and clicking down the stairs in her Louboutins before locking the exit door behind her with the keys that Deirdre had entrusted to her and stepping cautiously onto the slippery pavements.

Her silver Mini Cooper was parked just around the corner from the theatre and although the snow had now stopped falling, a white wedge had formed across her windscreen which necessitated her locating the ice scraper from the boot in order to clear her line of vision.

It took longer than anticipated and Erin, who rarely swore, found herself cursing as she sent chunks of hard snow crystal splattering into the air then climbed into the car, anxious for a guilty cigarette after so much unforeseen exertion.

But irritation piled upon frustration for now her warm breath was steaming up the windows so that she was forced to switch the air vent to maximum while waiting for the glass to clear. A cigarette would probably not help, so Erin sat impatiently drumming her long finger-nails against the steering wheel and dreaming of the heat of the Antipodean sunshine which she would be experiencing in just a few months.

It was then she noticed something not quite right about the windscreen. The other windows were clearing nicely but the windscreen still seemed cloudy and she would not risk driving off in such unpredictable weather until she was sure that she could see properly.

Her craving for nicotine having been rendered unadvisable, Erin pulled a box of tissues out of the glove compartment and flattened a handful against the glass, rubbing vigorously. She also made a serious mental note to go and see her mechanic as soon as she could and find out what was wrong with this car.

But the windscreen was still not clearing. In fact, if anything, it was worse. Now there appeared to be a kind of pattern forming which looked like letters, and her anger rose, convinced that some snotty-nosed kid had obviously been tampering with her car and had somehow managed to damage it.

Erin turned her wipers on to maximum speed, at a loss to know why, whatever was on the outside, should be so difficult to erase. She wondered whether the words had been put there not by fingers but with some sort of oily spray, for you never knew with vandals as they had no sense of respect for other people's property.

Feeling hot now and distinctly bothered, she got out of the car and tried to see what the defacer had written. She could just make out the letters I, O, I and T, then made a further attempt to clean the glass with yet more tissues while uttering a loud stream of expletives that would have made passers-by blush if there had been any around.

Finally, she gave up, returned to the car and rummaged in her bag for her cigarettes. With hands that were now far from steady, she lit one and dragged on it deeply before puffing out three perfect rings that rose slowly between her and the damned windscreen where she could now read the word clearly. TRIONFI.

It was a rubbish word and she had no idea what it meant. Was it French? Italian? But studying it again she realised that the letters appeared to have been written *inside* the car otherwise they wouldn't look like letters at all and the R, the N and the F would be the other way round.

Seriously unnerved, Erin slid an Ed Sheeran CD into her music player and fastened her seat-belt, determined to try and see past this obliteration for she only had to drive thirteen kilometres to her home and knew that it should take no longer than twenty minutes if the snow held off.

With her cigarette clenched between brightly glossed lips, she started the engine and strained her neck forward in order to concentrate on the road ahead. Turning on to the Ennis by-pass, she let out a relieved sigh for the motorway was straight and the glare from the oncoming cars was not such a distraction as it would be if she were travelling on any of the minor routes.

She tried to relax, visualising once again the rapturous applause and the stunning reviews that would be coming her way the following year. *"When my hair's all gone and my memory fades…"* crooned Ed as she put her foot down and increased her speed to a comfortable seventy.

The letters weren't bothering her any more. She was on the home stretch. This aggravating business had been just one of those blips in what had otherwise proved to be a successful day.

It was just past the Dromoland Inn and a few kilomotres short of her exit to Newmarket that Erin smelled burning. Mild at first like bread left a little too long in the toaster, then becoming stronger reminding her of charcoal but with a slight metallic odour that crept around her nostrils and down into her throat.

She dropped her speed and anxiously checked the ashtray. The cigarette that she had been smoking was well and truly out so what else could be causing such a powerful smell and which definitely seemed to be inside the car?

Her senses became immobilised, like a rabbit or a deer caught in the blaze of headlights, but she knew that she had to keep driving for there was no hard shoulder before her exit and she searched frantically for a slip road, anywhere that was safe to turn off and to try and locate the source of this latest wretched situation.

"Cause honey your soul can never grow old, it's evergreen..." Ed continued as her left hand groped around the passenger seat, touching her bag, her hat and her umbrella, anything that might have somehow caught a spark and that she could locate and toss out of the window if necessary. But there was nothing remotely visible that could be on fire and the caustic stench was now almost unbearable, so Erin slid open the windows, rasping out a deep cough while the letters on the windscreen, TRIONFI, grew bigger and bolder than ever, almost covering the glass.

Somehow, through watery eyes and smudged mascara, she crawled to a near standstill as other cars blasted their horns and shot past her, until, uttering a loud "Thank you, God", she finally saw a signpost indicating the way that led to the many loughs and nature walks in the area.

Without signalling, she turned the steering wheel hard left and swerved into the dark road, now panicked and anxious to park as soon as she was able, when she would ring the rescue service and ask them to collect her.

The road was narrow and winding, bordered by tall trees, and there were no other vehicles in sight as Erin carried slowly on until she could find a suitable place to stop. She tried to maintain optimism. At least she hadn't broken down and the lights were still working but she was sure now that there was something seriously wrong with the car that had she had always looked on as a reliable friend.

Then came the first in a succession of shocks which took her so totally by surprise that although her immediate impulse was to scream at the top of her lungs, she heard herself croak out an absurd and pitiable hauteur. "It's alright, Erin. It's alright."

A short dark figure that she could have sworn was human and not animal suddenly crossed from right to left in front of the car and then disappeared. Even though she was driving at a snail's pace, Erin stopped the car abruptly and sat in frozen silence, wondering what or who it was and considering whether she should get out and look. Had she hit it? She wasn't sure. But her instincts told her to put her foot down and despite the damaged windscreen and the smell she should not leave the car.

But before she could re-start the engine a sudden violent wind blew out of nowhere and hit the Mini full on. A gust that was so strong it carried the car and its passenger across to the left hand side of the road, up onto a small bank and smack into the trunk of an Ash tree where the sound of breaking glass precipitated the excrutiatingly slow dimming of the lights into total blackness.

Now she knew she was in serious trouble and bravado and optimism seemed hopelessly misplaced.

First, she groped in her bag for her i-phone and a light came on. Relieved, Erin punched out the number for the emergency services and when a female voice answered, she found herself gabbling in panic.

"Please give your location?" the voice asked again,

obviously unable to understand the torrent of hysteria-induced words.

"I'm…I'm in a road off the M.18, just before Newmarket. It's…it's where the lakes are. Come quickly please. I've crashed the car. It's dark…"

It took a few seconds to realise that the connection had failed and Erin heard herself shouting "No, no!" while shaking the phone furiously as if that would make the slightest difference, for there was no signal.

Perhaps the operator had heard enough to understand and send someone out. But then again…

The crash hadn't been bad enough to release the air bag so maybe the car would start.

Erin turned the key in the ignition and the engine spluttered for a brief moment, then died. She tried again but this time there wasn't even a click and she felt tears welling up in the back of her throat as she turned it again and again while sobbing loudly now in fear and frustration.

She knew she would have to get out of the car to inspect the damage. And also to find the large torch that she kept in the boot. Then she would make her way back towards the motorway where she would try and use her phone again or, out of desperation, hitch a lift.

Wiping her face with the back of her hand, Erin now resembled a macabre rag doll whose stitching had unravelled. She repeated to herself, less convincingly than before, that everything was going to be alright, although at the moment it was the stuff of nightmares and horror films. What was puzzling her was the fact that it was so dark. There was no moon and she couldn't even hear the motorway traffic, let alone see headlights, although she knew she had only driven a few hundred yards to where she was now and where she was experiencing the worst night of her life.

Tentatively, she stepped out of the car and realised that her right shoulder was throbbing horribly. It was true what they said, that fear could disguise pain, but in a way there was also a sense of renewal to be gained from being in the cold night air and she took several deep breaths as she groped in the back of the car for her torch. Then, when she had found it and switched it on, it was though its welcome beam had answered an unspoken prayer and delivered her from evil.

With the torch in one hand and her bag and phone clasped tightly in the other, Erin set off the way she had come and headed for the motorway wishing she had put boots on that morning instead of three inch heels. Pride before a fall, she thought miserably as she picked her way down the small bank that the car had mounted and started to walk along the narrow road.

The torch beam lit the road that lay ahead well and she swung it from side to side for she could not be sure whether the trees, now swaying like shadow dancers and unleashing powdery snow, were all her straining ears could decipher, or if there was something else that was watching and lying in wait for her.

At first she assumed it was a dead animal in the middle of the road, but as she nervously approached where the figure had crossed in front of the car, she saw what looked like a pile of dark rags. Hesitating, she peered closer, kicking her heel against the bundle to make sure, as the torch shone its light upon some soiled garments which seemed to be a combination of grey wool heaped upon taffeta.

Satisfied that it was just a bunch of old clothes, Erin stepped around it and was about to continue her journey when a sound brought her to a standstill once again.

This time she nearly vomited from fright. Could that really be a fiddle? A plaintive, soulful sound that cut through the blackness to play with her senses and eliminated every atom of constructive thought.

The music was familiar and yet she couldn't place where she had heard it before.

She stood rooted to the spot, the agonizing pain in her shoulder now the least of her worries. Who on God's green earth could be playing a fiddle in this remote place?

There were now only two choices that Erin could make and neither was good. She would walk on accompanied by this terrifying music and not knowing what other bizarre problems she might encounter, or return to the car, lock herself in and wait there until it was light. If the stench was still bad then she would live with it, for it had to be better than stepping into the dark unknown.

Moving as fast as her shoes would allow, Erin found herself moaning like the north Atlantic wind. Clambering up onto the bank towards the car the music seemed to swell around her as though someone had turned up the volume and it was now, with a sickening jolt, that she recognised it for the first time.

But – surely it couldn't be. How could the music used in the Arcanum finale be played here? But that was what it was for she had followed every note and knew it by heart.

Every nerve in her body on edge but clinging to the torch for grim death, Erin dropped her bag, pulled her car keys from her pocket and grappled with the lock, then with a cry of anguish hurled herself into the driver's seat, closing her eyes while she struggled to breathe normally and to relax her severely stressed muscles.

After a few seconds, she opened her eyes and that's when her piercing scream sliced through the night like the blade of Fergus. Even though the shock of what she was seeing caused her vision to swim around alarmingly, her brain still managed to absorb the pictures on the cards that were propped up against the windscreen inside the car and, in sheer disbelief, she leaned forward pointing the torch onto each and every one.

Twenty-two Tarot cards. All of the Major Arcana. They carried the look of age and even to Erin in her petrified state clearly bore only a passing resemblance to the costumes in the Arcanum set dance. The hues were more subtle than the bright designs that she had witnessed; rustic browns and tawny orange, sage green and violet against a background of sepia-tinted faded tapestry. The torchlight quivered as it shone on the faces of the characters: the blushed cheeks of the Magician, the sad countenance of the Fool, the hollow dark sockets of the eyes of Death.

She began to laugh then, her imagination relaying to her disturbed mind that she was the only Minor character present among a cast of Major trumps. Perhaps that was what someone was trying to tell her. That she had no chance of winning against such superior power.

Before she lost consciousness, Erin called loudly upon a God that she had forsaken to help her and not to allow her to die cold and alone in a strange place tormented by supernatural forces.

When dawn broke through a mass of heavy, grey clouds and the birds began to realise it was morning, the AA rescue service arrived to tow the Mini away while the paramedics carried the shaking woman from the car onto a stretcher and into a waiting ambulance.

Unlike Dennis Ahearne and many others in the world who had mentally obliterated extreme trauma, the choreographer remembered everything but refused to tell a soul lest she be considered insane.

Her work with Lighthouse would continue but there would be no Arcanum tribute show for she had learned to dread even the mention of the word Tarot. Instead, she would re-wind and play back every detail of her ordeal from the moment she stepped out of the theatre that evening to when unconsciousness thankfully claimed her, and those memories were to remain through every dream and nightmare that Erin Shaw was to experience for the rest of her life.

★

EPILOGUE.
CO. CLARE. 1785

The old woman nodded with satisfaction at the choice she had made.

He was an upstanding young man with a fine reputation

who had tutored Set and Ceili dances around the counties of Galway and Limerick and who was now watching with fascinated interest the diverse assembly of individuals whom he had inherited.

She noted that he gazed with surprised delight as they incorporated unparalleled arm and foot movements into their dances and he gasped at the flying jumps they were performing on the hard ground. She was also heartened that he appeared admiring of their diligence which she was certain he would endeavour to continue to nurture.

And he wore the coat, hat and shoes as if they had been made especially for him, respecting that they were on loan together with the silver-topped cane for as long as he was a guest in their county.

This impression lasted but a few minutes and she resisted a volcanic urge to remain longer, slowly making her way back down the hill, past the silver mirror lake, resting now and then on her hazel staff and looking back whenever the fiddler played a particular air evoking memories that were long out of season.

The woman pulled her grey shawl tighter around her thin arms as the first chill of autumn transformed itself into a dense cloud that curled its way down from the mountains and through the thick forest.

As it drifted towards her, she gave a secret smile, satisfied that her work here was done, then touching her golden cross with a prayer, allowed the mist which held so many secrets to once again take her at its will.

A POTTED HISTORY OF THE IRISH DANCE.

Irish dance dates back to traditions in Ireland in the 1500's and is closely tied to Irish independence and cultural identity. Through history, these ancient dances were never documented or recorded due to Ireland's occupation by England, which tried to make Ireland more "English" by outlawing certain traditional practices. Many Irish cultural traditions were banned by the English authorities duringthe 400-year period that came to be known as the Penal Days.

Despite this ban on cultural traditions in Ireland, Irish dancing continued behind closed doors. Because their musical instruments had been confiscated by the authorities, Irish parents taught their children the dances by tapping out rhythms with their hands and feet and making music through "lilting" (or mouth music somewhat similar to "scat singing" in jazz). Irish dances came from Ireland's family clans and, like tribal Native American dances in the U.S.A were never formally choreographed or recorded.

But we do have some idea of the dances done by the Irish in the mid-1500s. These would have included Rinnce Fada or Fading where two lines with partners faced each other, Irish Hey (possibly a round or figure dance), jigs (likely in a group), Trenchmores (described as a big free form country dance), and sword dances. English suppression of Irish culture continued, exemplified by the banning of piping and the arrest of pipers. However, Queen Elizabeth I was "exceedingly pleased" with Irish tunes and country dances.

Power struggles between the Irish and English continued

during the 1600s. The Penal Laws enacted in the late 1600s crushed Irish commerce and industries. The laws also banned the education of Catholic children leading to hidden (hedge) schools. Traditional Irish culture was practiced with some degree of secrecy. This period of severe repression lasted for more than a hundred years, explaining some of the initial secrecy of teaching Irish step dancing. The Church itself sometimes condemned dancing stating that "In the dance are seen frenzy and woe."

A major influence on Irish dance and Irish culture was the advent of the Dance Masters around 1700 beginning a tradition that you could argue continues today. A dance master typically travelled within a county, stopping in a village and sometimes staying with a hospitable family (who were honored by their selection as host). They taught Irish dancing (male teachers) in kitchens, farm outbuildings, crossroads, or hedge schools. Students would first learn the jig and reel. Sometimes, the teacher had to tie a rope around a student's leg to distinguish right foot from left. Besides dancing, they also appear to have given instruction in fencing and other skills. Some teachers had other skilled trades that were used on occasion by the villagers, helping to explain dance masters habit of traveling from town to town. Having an eminent dance master associated with your village was a cause for pride and boasting by the community.

Each dance master had a repertoire of dance steps and he created new steps over time. (Eight measures or bars of music are called a "step," hence the term step dancing.) These men were the creators of the set and ceili dances and they carefully guarded their art of step creation. Dance masters created the first schools of dancing, the best known being from Counties Kerry, Cork, and Limerick. One dance master described himself as "an artificial rhythmical walker" and "instructor of youth in the Terpsichorean art." Villagers paid dance masters at the end of the third week of teaching at a "benefit night." They paid the accompanying musician a week later. Sometimes, the dance master was both musician and dancer simultaneously! Apparently the level of pay for the dance masters was relatively high for Ireland and it included room and board.

The Penal Laws were finally lifted in the late 1800's, inspiring Irish nationalism and the Great Gaelic Revival—the resurgence of interest in Irish language, literature, history and folklore—and its accompanying feis (essentially a gathering that included various forms of competition). The feis was typically held in open fields and included contests in singing, playing music, baking, and, or course, Irish dancing.

In 1929, the Irish Dancing Commission was founded (An Coimisiun le Rinci' Gaelacha) to establish rules regarding teaching, judging, and competitions. It continues in that role. Prior to 1929, many local variations in dances, music, costumes and the rules of feisianna existed. Part of the impact of the Commission was standardization of competitions.

During the 20th Century, Irish dance has evolved in terms of locations, costumes, and dance technique. For example, during the period of the dance masters, stages were much smaller including table tops, half doors, and sometimes the "stage" was simply a crossroad. (An old poem called dancing "tripping the sod.") Tests of dancing ability involved dancing on the top of a barrel or on a soaped table! As stages became larger, the dance changed in at least two ways. The movement of dancers across a stage increased greatly (a judge would now subtract points if a dancer did not "use the stage"), and dance steps that require substantial space became possible (e.g., "flying jumps"). The location of competitions also changed over time from barns or outdoors where flat bed trucks were used as stages, to predominately indoors in hotels, schools or fairgrounds.

Irish dance has evolved in other ways during the 20th Century. Instruction is beginning at a younger age. Who is instructed has also changed from mostly males to mostly females (the turning point was before 1930). Girls dancing solos in competition were rare before the 1920s. Dance styles have also changed; for example, arms and hands are not always held rigid during solo dances. Some argue that stiff arms were less provocative, others that the Church was trying to increase dancers' self control. Hand movements still occur in figure (group) dances.

In 1969, the Irish Dance World Championships started in Dublin, and competitive Irish dancing continued to gain momentum. As the students of the first generation of dance masters became established in America in the 1970's, the first American Irish step dancing champions began to emerge, and would change the art form forever.

THE BOOK *EVERYONE'S* TALKING ABOUT!
CURRENTLY RATED *FIVE STARS*
ON AMAZON

'A cracking first novel'

Matthew Cain, Arts Editor, Channel 4